A Tear in the Sky

Sky

The Templar Chronicles
Book Three

JOSEPH NASSISE

Second Edition

A Tear in the Sky © 2007 by Joseph Nassise
Jacket artwork © 2010 Neil Jackson

Harbinger Books
Phoenix, Arizona

CHAPTER 1

"ANCIENT ENEMIES"

THE PRIEST RAN TOWARD THE altar as if hell itself followed on his heels.

He didn't have much time, minutes at best. Still, that might be enough. The others would have a warning at least. It was the best he could do, given the circumstances.

Racing up the steps, he crossed to the tabernacle and spun the dials on the lock with trembling fingers. He set the second one incorrectly and had to do it again, losing precious seconds in the process. Opening the tabernacle, he bent one knee, genuflected, and then removed the ciborium from inside the blessed chamber.

From the other end of the church he could hear them banging on the inside of the sacristy door. He'd locked it behind him, but he didn't expect it to hold them for long.

Opening the ciborium and removing one of the communion wafers, he begged for Christ's forgiveness for his sins and then placed the wafer on his tongue. From years past the voice of

Father Jerome, his old seminary professor, came to him.

"Viaticum, from the Latin 'via tecum', meaning 'provisions for the journey.' The final rite in the sacrament of Extreme Unction, the giving of the Eucharist ensures that the dying do not die alone, but have Christ with them in their final moments just as He has been with them in life."

Behind him, the door to the sacristy burst from its hinges and the howls of his pursuers filled the nave.

He was out of time.

Steeling himself for what he knew was to come, he calmly closed the tabernacle and spun the dials, locking it against intrusion. It wouldn't hold out a determined thief, but he had done his part and could rest easy on that score. He got to his feet and turned to face the front of the church.

The shadows had reached the transept.

He hurried to the altar and took up the Bible resting there. It wouldn't hold them off but he felt better with it in his hands.

As they reached the foot of the altar, he calmly went down to meet them.

CHAPTER 2

"MONSTERS AND MESSAGES"

K NIGHT COMMANDER CADE WILLIAMS STALKED down the hallway of the Bennington Containment Facility, angry at himself for being there yet knowing that he really had no choice in the matter.

Just hours before a request had been relayed to him by the facility's warden. The request had originated from the prison's most high-profile prisoner, Simon Logan, the Necromancer, a man who had used the arcane power in the Spear of Longinus to try to destroy the Order itself.

He would have succeeded, too, if it hadn't been for Cade and the men of the Echo Team.

Logan had apparently asked to see Cade. Said it was urgent even. But it was the note that accompanied the request that had captured his attention.

Just eight simple words.

I have a message from your wife, Gabrielle.

Anything else the Necromancer might have said would have been ignored outright. After turning Logan over to those who ran the facility, Cade's interest in the former head of the Council of Nine had vanished. He had other, more pertinent things to worry about than the fate of a man who had tried to take on the Order and lost.

But if Logan had actually received a message from Cade's long dead wife, Gabrielle, then that was something Cade couldn't simply ignore. As a necromancer, Logan certainly had an affinity for the dead, which made the possibility that he'd spoken to Gabrielle a realistic one.

Cade knew his wife's spirit was not at rest. He'd encountered her shade several times over the last few months and it was Gabrielle herself who had convinced Cade not to slay Logan outright when he'd been at Cade's mercy following the assault on the Council's stronghold. Why she might have relayed a message through the Necromancer rather than simply coming to see him herself was what he didn't understand and that lack of understanding was what had driven him to agree to the visit.

He reached the guard station at the end of the hall. There he surrendered his side arm, watch, and the contents of his pockets. The black feather he wore on a piece of leather about his neck was glanced at curiously when he laid it down with the rest of his items, but no one made any comment. One of the guards requested that Cade remove his gloves, but the senior officer stepped in and informed the guard that that wouldn't be necessary.

Which was good because Cade wouldn't have agreed to the request anyway. His gloves stayed on, no matter where he went. He wouldn't have objected to giving up the eye patch that covered the ruin of his right eye, but they didn't ask.

He waited with the senior officer for the junior one to buzz them through the gate and then the two men moved down the end of the hall and through a series of three more barriers until they came to the room outside the Necromancer's cell.

Cade was a member of the Holy Order of the Poor Knights of Christ of the Temple of Solomon, or the Knights Templar, as they were once more commonly known. Long thought to have been destroyed in the fourteenth century, the Templars had emerged from hiding during the desperate days of World War II and had joined with the very entity that had excommunicated them en-masse so many centuries before, the Catholic Church. Reborn as a secret military arm of the Vatican, the Templars were now charged with defending mankind from the supernatural in all its forms.

As the commander of the Echo Team, the most prestigious of the elite strike units fielded by the Templars, Cade was known for both his ruthless efficiency and his often unorthodox methods.

The two men guarding the Necromancer recognized him by sight, despite the fact that he'd never been down to this part of the maximum security level before, and were already opening up the doors to the room beyond as he stepped up to the guard station.

The man who'd escorted him turned to face him. "Rule #1: Nothing goes in that doesn't come out. Rule #2: No physical contact with the prisoner. And Rule #3: If you need help, just yell and we'll come running. Got it?"

Cade nodded and then stepped through the door.

The room was large, about twelve feet to a side, and in its center stood a cage of iron. The cage had been home to Simon Logan, the man known as the Necromancer, ever since Cade had defeated him in battle several months ago. It was furnished with a bed, a toilet, and a small writing desk, nothing more.

Inside the cage waiting for him was the Necromancer.

Logan was a shadow of his former self. He'd lost considerable weight, his features sinking into the ruin of his face like a pumpkin past its prime, his bones poking awkwardly against the confines of his jumpsuit. He was in constant movement, shuffling back and forth across the small space of his cell, eight steps across and then eight steps back, over and over again, like a man hunted by something he couldn't see nor understand.

His first words to Cade seemed to reinforce that viewpoint.

"The dead torment me."

His voice was a reedy whisper, so different from the bold commands he'd shouted at his followers before his defeat.

Cade had no sympathy for him. "As well they should," he replied. Logan had thought nothing of dragging the souls of the dead back across the barrier between the land of the dead and that of the living and forcing them to reanimate their decomposed and corrupted bodies. For him to be haunted by those he'd treated in such a fashion was nothing but justice itself and Cade told him so.

Logan went on as if he hadn't heard.

"They torment me. Especially *her*."

Cade's pulse quickened.

"Who?" he asked.

"You know who."

Cade crossed the room to stand in front of Logan. For all he knew Logan was running an elaborate con and so Cade refused to give him anything. "No, I don't," he said, "tell me."

Logan's response, when it came, surprised him.

"She said you wouldn't believe me, so she said to give you this."

As Logan reached inside the pocket of his prison uniform, Cade automatically braced for an attack, expecting him to pull out a shiv or some other makeshift weapon he'd fashioned without the guards' knowledge. But Logan's hand emerged from the interior of his clothing with only a pewter medallion that dangled from a silver chain.

Logan tossed the necklace through the bars at Cade.

Wary of arcane trickery, Cade refused to catch it, stepping back and letting it fall to the floor at his feet.

A glance downward told him it was a Saint Christopher medallion, the kind a lot of cops carried around, Christopher being the patron saint of policemen and lost causes.

This particular medal had a dent in it, right in the center where the face of the saint had once been, a dent large enough that it obliterated the saint's entire image, leaving just the caption running around the outside of the disk.

Seeing it, Cade froze.

He recognized that dent. Remembered the night that medallion had deflected a bullet that should have take his head off like it was yesterday, how that tiny piece of medal had saved his life and consequently the life of his partner as well. They'd been pinned down in a shadowy corridor inside a Southie tenement house and had never even seen their assailant until that shot had come blazing out of the darkness. Saint Christopher had saved his life, there was no question of that, and he'd worn that medallion night and day for years afterwards in a superstitious show of faith.

Cade's heart beat wildly. A hand reached out in front of him and it took him a moment to realize it was his own. He picked the medallion up and turned it over, knowing even before he did so what he would see.

The inscription read: "Every day after this is a gift. Use them well."

He'd put it there, the day after the shooting, to remind him just how fragile and transitory life actually was. He'd never taken the medallion off, not until that horrible summer day seven years ago.

Cade's fist clenched around the medallion.

"Where did you get this?" he asked, his voice as cold as winter snow.

But Logan didn't even flinch. He simply stared at Cade with those eyes that had seen too much and said, "She said you'd suspect that I'd taken it from her grave, so she gave me a message for you."

Cade visibly started. It was as if Logan were reading his mind. He had been thinking that Logan, or at least one of his cronies, had disturbed Gabrielle's rest and he was ready to tear the man limb from limb for doing so.

"One day at a time. She told me to tell you one day at a time."

A wave of dizziness washed over him at the implications of what Logan was saying. Seven years ago he'd put that same Saint Christopher medallion in his wife's hand just before the funeral director had closed the casket over her still and silent form. Call it superstitious, but he'd wanted her to have some extra protection in the next life, considering how horribly this one had ended for her. He vividly remembered leaning down to kiss her cold cheek and whispering to her, asking her how he was going to survive without her.

She'd apparently decided to finally answer his question.

Cade stayed lost in thought for several long moments. At last he looked up and met Logan's eager gaze. "I'm listening," he said.

Logan seemed to gain some of his old confidence back at Cade's reaction. He stepped away from the bars, went back to pacing back and forth across the space of his cell. "I have some requests," he began, but Cade cut him off.

"I don't have time to play games, Logan. Get to the point."

The Necromancer turned to face him.

"Sunlight."

"I'm sorry?" The comment was so unexpected that Cade had trouble following the other man's train of thought.

"Sunlight. I want to see sunlight again, before the end of my trial."

Cade didn't have to even think about it. He knew the prisoner was going to be transferred from Bennington to Longfort at the end of the month and doing so would require him to travel in an armored transport vehicle. The transport had windows. Provided it didn't rain on the day he made the trip, Cade knew he could persuade the warden to forget the blindfold and let the prisoner have one last look at the sunlight, though why Logan would want it was beyond Cade's ability to fathom. No matter. He'd put a window in Logan's personal cell if that was what it would take to get the information he needed out of him, orders to the contrary be damned.

"Done," Cade replied. "Sunlight. Before the end of your trial."

Logan grinned slyly, but Cade pretended not to see it. "Now," he said instead, "tell me what she said."

Logan explained that Gabrielle's shade was visiting him every night, tormenting him, refusing to let him sleep. "She just keeps repeating the same refrain, over and over again, her voice like an ice pick in my mind." He closed his eyes, as if he wanted to avoid any distractions and get it right.

"The Lady in the Tower sleeps beneath the banner of night on the island of lost dreams, but her sleep is not restful and she can find no peace."

"What the hell does that mean?"

"I would think it would be obvious, Commander."

"So wow me with your superior knowledge."

"Your wife is not dead, simply a captive of the Adversary."

Cade stood there, stunned.

It was perhaps the last thing he'd ever expected to hear. And yet, somehow, he suspected that the Necromancer was right.

Gabrielle? Alive?

That put a whole new perspective on things.

CHAPTER 3

"A FAR, FAR BETTER REST"

C ADE SPENT THE NEXT THREE days wrestling with his thoughts, trying to come to grips with the doubts that had arisen in the aftermath of his conversation with the Necromancer. They had burrowed deep within the heart of him, their questing tendrils seeking out the soft places of his soul and anchoring there like some kind of cancerous mass, growing roots, oozing outward unchecked, until they were so large that ignoring them was no longer even an option. Not knowing would eat him alive, would consume him from the inside out. There was no other choice; he would have to see for himself.

For that, he was going to need some help.

Later that afternoon he knocked on the door to Riley's quarters in the senior noncoms housing unit. "I could use your help," Cade said to him without preamble when Riley opened the door.

The other man shrugged. "Sure. Anything you need."

"You might want to hear me out first," said Cade and something in his voice made Riley do just that.

Cade had his personal vehicle there at the commandery and so the two of them took a leisurely afternoon drive, wandering the back roads as Cade laid out the problem and exactly what he intended to do.

Riley was silent as Cade talked, letting him get it all out without interruption, but when he was finished Riley didn't hold anything back.

"You know Logan's a lying son-of-a-bitch, don't you? That he's probably telling you all this just to mess with your head?"

Cade nodded. "That was my first reaction. But what if he's not?"

"What do you mean 'what if he's not'? Of course he is! He's the freakin' Necromancer. Lying is all that he does."

"Maybe. And maybe not. But I can't take that chance. If there is even the slightest possibility that some part of what he told me is the truth, then I need to find out. And there is only one way of doing that."

Riley shook his head. "What you're proposing is nuts. It's public property and the cops are always cruising by the place. You wouldn't last twenty minutes."

Cade shrugged. "Doesn't matter. I don't have any choice. I've got to try and see for myself. I'm going nuts second guessing it all."

Riley didn't reply.

They continued driving in silence for a time, each of them lost in their own thoughts. The December landscape unfolded around them, empty fields and stark, barren trees that reached outward with skeletal branches, the road winding up and down, around this hill and over that, headed everywhere and nowhere.

Cade knew the idea was risky, and he had no desire to try explaining everything to the police should they be caught, but he was willing to take that chance. The only issue was whether his friend was willing to go along with it.

After a long while, Cade spoke up. "So, are you in or not?"

Riley looked over at him. "Of course I'm in."

And at that, Cade just had to smile.

* * *

It was a simple headstone, plain grey New Hampshire granite, its front polished to a glistening shine so that the words carved into its face contrasted sharply with the smooth surface. Unlike the other stones around it, this one did not contain a name. Nor was there the usual assemblage of dates. Cade had not seen the need for them; he knew who rested here, knew when she had been born and the awful day that she'd died. He didn't need a set of dates to remind him of those times. He'd known that he'd be the only one returning here after the funeral was over and he'd chosen to leave them off the marker. In their place he had selected a line from Dickens that seemed particularly appropriate to him during those dark summer days immediately following Gabrielle's death.

It is a far, far better rest I go to,
than I have ever known

Now, looking at those words in the pale light from his flashlight, he was struck with an overwhelming sense of bitterness. What foolish arrogance had made him choose that quote over some other? Rest was certainly the last thing she had received and he suspected that it was all his fault.

"Are you sure you want to do this?" Riley asked. Cade knew it was his friend's way of giving him one last chance to think about the potential consequences, but he'd already made up his mind. He had to know. It was as simple as that.

In answer to Riley's question, Cade picked up his shovel, drove it deep into the earth in front of the headstone, and began digging.

Riley watched him for a moment and then joined in.

They worked in companionable silence, save for the sound their shovels made biting into the dirt and the whispering of the wind through the trees around them like a watchful taskmaster urging them on. The recent rains had softened the earth, but all the moisture it retained made it heavier and Cade soon found himself sweating from the effort. His only focus was getting to the casket below so that he could quench the growing sense of urgency unfurling in his gut.

They piled the dirt beside the grave, knowing they were going to need it again before they were done. Its rich full scent filled Cade's nostrils and he thought it strange how the aroma of life could be found here even surrounded by so much death. The work was hard, the dirt heavy and seemingly unwilling to reveal that which it hid from prying eyes. A backhoe would have made the effort far easier, but Cade dared not risk it. This was a public cemetery, after all, and the machine would only call attention to them. A passerby might miss a pair of men digging in the glow of a flashlight but ignoring a bright yellow piece of earth moving equipment was another story entirely. Getting caught was the last thing Cade wanted to happen; grave robbery had a fairly serious sentence attached to it. He'd taken as many precautions as he could think of. They'd parked his Cherokee in the woods a couple hundred yards away from the cemetery entrance and had cut through the woods until they'd reached the stone fence that surrounded the property. They'd clambered up and over it and from there made their way through the maze of headstones until they'd come to the secluded area where Gabrielle had been laid to rest. It was in the rear quarter of the cemetery, as far from the road as it was possible to get, and their flashlights had been covered with red filters to limit their visibility.

Two hours after they started, Riley's shovel hit something hard, something that wasn't dirt. He drew the shovel out of the ground and pushed it back in again, this time a few feet to the left of his previous strike. Another dull thud came back to them.

`They worked a bit more quickly after that, reenergized by the discovery, and it wasn't long before the top of the casket was revealed, its black lacquer surface, so polished and shiny the last time Cade had laid eyes on it, now dulled from the patina of dirt that coated it. Once the lid was uncovered it took only a short burst of effort to clear the earth away from the sides of the casket, giving them room to open it. As Riley climbed out of the hole to get the necessary tools, Cade got down on his knees and examined the lid. Even in the limited light of his flashlight he could tell at once that it was still sealed shut, just as it had been in the day it had been lowered into the ground.

As he waited, Cade's thoughts turned to what was before him. Gabrielle's death had not been an easy one. The damage the Adversary had done to her face had been horrible. In the autopsy that followed, a legal requirement in the case of a homicide, the medical examiner had been unable to determine a specific cause of death. The idea that a mortician would continue the process the ME had begun, heaping further indignities on her earthly remains, had been more than Cade could bear and he'd had her immediately buried without even the benefit of being embalmed, just wanting to get the whole process over with as quickly as possible. To be certain the funeral home carried out his wishes, he insisted on being present throughout the preparation process and had them seal the casket in front of him.

Now, seven years later, he knew little would remain of the woman he had once held so lovingly in his arms. The human body began decomposing shortly after death and nature was remarkably efficient at the process of tearing it down. Cade knew that within just a few weeks the hair, teeth, and nails become detached from the rest of the body, the body itself swells with gases, the skin splits open, and the tissues begin to liquefy. After about a year all that's left are a bare skeleton and teeth.

As Cade cleaned the last of the dirt from the lid of the coffin, Riley jumped back down into the pit, a pair of tire irons in hand.

"Are you ready?" he asked.

Nothing but dust and bones, Cade thought, *dust and bones. I can handle that.*

The lock on the casket wasn't a typical pin and tumbler device but actually a simple cranking mechanism. A narrow key, similar to an Allen wrench, was inserted into the lock and then the key was turned several times to crank down the lid and seal it tightly. Cade had no doubt that moisture from the spring rains and melting winter snow had gotten into the lock over the years, corroding the interior, sealing together the moving parts deep in the core, and so he hadn't even bothered trying to get his hands on a proper casket key. Instead, he'd brought along a battery-powered electric drill and he used it now to drill out the lock itself, driving deep holes into the center of the mechanism, effectively rendering it useless.

When he was finished, Riley handed him one of the two

crowbars they had brought with them and each man took up a position on either side of lock with about three feet between them. Inserting the flat ends of their wedges into the thin space along the rubber seal between the side of the casket and the lid, they counted to three aloud and then pushed down with all their weight.

At first the lid resisted their effort to open it. But after working at it for several long minutes, they began to make some headway. Finally, there was a sharp crack as the lock broke and the lid jumped open a few inches before coming back down to rest against the edge of their crowbars.

Riley stepped back a few feet, giving Cade some distance out of respect for what he had to do, and for that Cade was grateful. Cade put down the crowbar, placed both hands on the lid, bracing himself for what was to come. Gathering his courage, he said a quick prayer for forgiveness, and then pushed the lid fully open.

For a long moment all he could do was stare. Somewhere in the back of his mind he dimly registered Riley's whispered "Mary, Mother of God!" but he didn't acknowledge it. He couldn't have, even if he'd wanted to, for what lay in front of him had stripped him of his ability to do anything but stare in shocked amazement.

His wife Gabrielle's body lay inside the casket just as it had on the day they'd sealed it away, perfectly preserved and without even the faintest hint of decomposition or decay. It was as if she belonged in some storybook fairytale, Sleeping Beauty or Snow White or some such, the princess resting peacefully on the bed of white silk that lined the casket, dressed in the sky blue summer dress that Cade had selected for her so long ago. Her hair shone as though a brush had been run through those auburn tresses only moments before and her skin was firm and taut, just as it had been in life. Her good eye was still closed, adding to the illusion that she was just sleeping, and it was so perfect, so real, that Cade found himself reaching out with one hand, intent on checking for a pulse, half-believing for just a moment that maybe she wasn't dead, that there had been some horrible mistake and that she had been waiting here all this time for him to come and rescue here.

Reality came rushing back in with a crash, as his gaze landed on the thick piece of gauze that had been used to cover the other side of her face, the side that the Adversary had sloughed the skin from, leaving the tissue and muscles beneath exposed to the light, and on the end of the autopsy incision that could just been seen near the scooped neckline of her dress. Gabrielle was dead, Cade knew that, knew it with the certainty of one who has loved and lost, and yet...and yet something clearly wasn't right here.

"What sorcery is this?" Riley asked, stepping back up next to Cade so as to get a better look at the tableau laid out before him.

Sorcery indeed Cade thought, and he knew that Riley had it right in one. Sorcery was exactly what had happened here, sorcery of the type that only a creature as powerful as the Adversary could pull off. With a sudden flash of understanding, Cade reached up and pulled the eye patch off his right eye. He turned his bad eye just so, activating his Sight, and the shimmering web of arcane energies that surrounded his wife's body sprang into view, wrapping her so deeply in their depths that she resembled a spider's prey encased in a cocoon.

Cade let Riley know what he was seeing.

"This is not good, boss, not good at all," the big master sergeant said and for the first time that night there was a hint of fear in his tone.

"Tell me about it," Cade muttered back in reply, still examining the black glistening bands of energy that shimmered with power in front of his eyes. He'd never seen anything like them and considering all the strange and unusual things he'd dealt with in the years since he'd joined the Order that was saying a lot.

"What are you going to do?"

"I'm taking her home," Cade replied, hesitantly at first, and then with more conviction. "Yes, taking her home."

Riley ran a dirty hand over his bald head. "Man, I don't know," he said. He started pacing in the small space in front of the unearthed casket. "You sure that's a good idea?"

Cade laughed and there wasn't anything close to humor in it. "Of course it's not a good idea. But what else am I going to do? Leave her here? Just cover her up again and pretend that I don't know anything about it? Not bloody likely!"

"Damn it, Cade, for all you know she's some kind of ticking time bomb, waiting until she's close enough to her target before going off with a bang. You can't bring that kind of power into the commandery without knowing more about it."

Cade shook his head. "I don't intend to. I'm not talking about bringing her back to the commandery, I'm talking about taking her home. To my place. I can put her in the workshop, get someone I know to erect a series of wards around her. That way, if anything does happen, it will be confined within the bounds of a sacred circle, limiting its impact."

"How do you even know it's safe to touch her?"

Cade gave that one some thought. His Sight hadn't manifested itself until several weeks after Gabrielle's funeral, so he hadn't known anything about the mysterious web of power before unearthing her body, but he suspected that whatever it was, it had been there since the moment the Adversary had snatched her life away. Which meant that the police, the coroner, and even the funeral home staff had touched her without disturbing it and that reinforced Cade's suspicion that he could do the same. Impulsively, he reached out toward her and Riley's shouted "No!" but wasn't in time to stop Cade from laying his hand upon Gabrielle's.

CHAPTER 4

"STEALING THE DEAD"

H ER SKIN WAS WARM.
So warm that Cade could feel its heat even through the thin cotton gloves that he habitually wore.

It was utterly unexpected and Cade snatched his hand back, swearing beneath his breath.

"What is it?" Riley asked, and when Cade turned to face him, he found Riley standing with his gun pointed at the casket, his gaze jumping back and forth between Gabrielle's body and Cade himself.

"Her skin," Cade said, "It's…warm."

"Warm?" Riley asked, his thumb stealing along the butt of his pistol and flicking the safety off as he turned to give the casket and what it contained his full attention.

Cade pushed the muzzle of the gun downward. "It's okay," he said, holding up his other hand in a calming gesture, "it just surprised me is all. I wasn't expecting it."

Riley still looked uneasy, but he deferred to Cade's judgment.

Cade reached in, sliding his hands beneath his wife's body, and lifted her carefully out of the casket. Her body was soft and pliant, like she had simply fallen asleep rather than been dead and buried for seven long years. Feelings Cade had never adequately dealt with came rushing back, threatening to overwhelm him.

Focus, man, focus.

Turning, he passed Gabrielle up to Riley, who placed her gently in the grass a few feet away as Cade climbed out of the grave. The two men picked up the shovels and got to work, filling in the grave as quickly as they could, conscious that if they were discovered now it would be disastrous.

Filling in the hole took a lot less time than digging it had and it wasn't long before they were winding their way back between the headstones, Riley carrying the tools and leading the way while Cade followed behind with Gabrielle's body slung over one shoulder in a fireman's carry. When they reached the stone wall that marked the burial ground's perimeter, Riley tossed the tools one at a time over the top. The 'clank' they made as they landed in the gravel on the other side seemed unnaturally loud in the night's stillness. They waited a moment to see if anything came of it and when nothing did, Riley boosted himself up onto the wall and then disappeared over the other side.

It was about a ten minute walk back to where they'd left the Jeep, which meant Cade had some time along with Gabrielle before Riley returned. He sat with her in his arms, his back against the wall, and talked to her. Told her how much he loved her. How much he missed her. How sorry he was that he hadn't searched for her before this and of how he would do anything to release her from whatever strange sorcery held her in its grip. His tears flowed freely.

A few moments later Riley was back, a blanket and coil of rope he'd taken from the back of Cade's truck in hand.

Riley tossed the blanket over the wall to Cade, who used it to wrap up Gabrielle's body. While Riley held on to one end of the rope, Cade wound the other end around the blanket-wrapped form, tied it securely off, and then climbed up astride the wall where he guided the bundle up the side of the wall as Riley hauled on the rope from the other side. Once the body reached the top, Cade lifted it over the edge and then passed it down to Riley, who was waiting below.

Riley picked up the tools and then led the way through the woods as Cade followed behind him carrying Gabrielle. It didn't take them long and both men breathed a sigh of relief once Gabrielle's body was secured beneath a blanket in the rear compartment.

The ride itself passed without incident. Arriving at his home, Cade drove around behind the house to his workshop, a two story barn that he had gutted and remodeled shortly after buying the property. He turned the Jeep around in the drive and backed it up close to the entrance. His neighbors were half a mile away on either side, far enough that the chances of being seen were slim in the middle of the day, never mind the dead of night, but Cade had learned to be cautious. The two men maneuvered Gabrielle's body out of the back of the Jeep and carried it inside.

What had once been horse stables was now a large, open room with bookshelves lining the walls and several work tables arranged in a semi-circle facing toward the door. A wood-burning stove stood in the far corner, its thick black pipe running up through the floor of the second story high above.

Cade caught Riley's glance at the throw rug in the center of the room between the tables, where a large mirror had been hidden only a few weeks before.

"Don't worry, it's gone." Cade said.

The mirror had served its purpose, allowing Cade regular travel into the Beyond while he searched for his wife's shade, but it had almost killed him too. If it hadn't been for Riley's timely arrival on that night less than a month before, he would have died from hunger and thirst, the prolonged travel in and out of the Beyond having depleted his body's natural resources without him being aware of it. Riley had called in the cavalry, rushing him by helicopter to the nearby Ravensgate Commandery and into the care of the best physicians the Order had on call.

Cade still wasn't exactly clear about who or what had miraculously cured him while in the hospital, but there was no doubt that it had been a supernatural event. He had vague memories of a hooded figure standing over his bedside but that was all. At the time he'd suspected Sergeant Duncan of using his own unusual powers to heal him, but the younger soldier swore adamantly that he had nothing to do with it when confronted later about the issue.

They carried Gabrielle's body over to the couch and laid her down gently.

"You want me to get a few of our mystics over here?" Riley asked, reaching for the cell phone on his belt.

Cade shook his head. "I'd rather keep the Order out of this for as long as I can."

"But I thought you were going to have the place warded?"

"I am. I'm just not going to use the Order's mystics to do it."

Riley thought about that one for a moment, then, "Okay. I

suspect this is one of those things that I don't really want to know, right?"

Cade lifted his hands in a "what can I say?" gesture.

Over the years Cade had cultivated various contacts outside the approved ranks of those the Order considered allies and he used them whenever necessary, despite the fact that doing so was against the Rule. Riley was aware of the practice and even condoned it in certain situations, but he preferred to remain ignorant of the details unless it was absolutely necessary that he be brought into the loop.

"That's fine with me. Just get those wards up as soon as possible."

"I will. You can trust me on that."

Riley grunted, glanced once more at Gabrielle, and then moved toward the door.

"Matt?"

Riley turned and faced him.

"Thanks. I owe you one."

The other man smiled at last. "You owe me so many I've lost count. But you're welcome anyway."

* * *

About an hour after Riley left there was a soft knock on the workshop door. When Cade opened it, a dark-haired woman slipped inside and moved to the center of the room.

"Thanks for coming so quickly, Denise," Cade said as she marched past him without even a hello. She was a fit woman in her late twenties, dressed simply in jeans, a pull-over sweatshirt, and hiking boots. Her brown hair was pulled back with a rubber band, but Cade could still see a streak of green and blue here and there. A green Army surplus satchel hung from a strap over her shoulder.

She waved away his thanks, her gaze moving about the room, searching. When she didn't find what she was looking for, she turned to face him.

"Where is she?"

Trying to keep the grin of amusement at her single-minded focus off his face, Cade inclined his head toward the stairs. "Spare bedroom, last door on the left."

Denise Clearwater was a witch. A hedge witch, actually. Able to use the power inherent in Nature to bend reality to her will. Nothing drastic, just a nudge here and there, when time and circumstance demanded it. He'd met her several years before when Echo was forced to deal with a nest of minor demons that tried to lay claim to Long Island. Operating on the age-old principle that the enemy of my enemy is my friend, Cade had agreed to an alliance with Clearwater and her coven. With the two groups working in conjunction with each other, they were able to isolate and ultimately banish the infernal creatures back to their own realm. Clearwater herself had set the wards that would keep the portal from opening again for another thousand years and it was her obvious mastery of that talent that had brought her to mind when he found himself in his present circumstances.

Without knowing exactly what the Adversary had done to Gabrielle, Cade didn't dare have her body in his home without some kind of protection around it. A set of wards seemed to be just what the situation called for.

Designed to guard a specific location or object, wards were one of the mainstays of modern magick. They came in two types; minor and major. Minor wards were just what the name inferred;

minor magicks that could be used to protect an object or a location for the short term. These could be performed by a single individual with limited preparation, often on the fly. Major wards were another story entirely, intended to last indefinitely and requiring several days of preparation by a sorcerer with considerable power, using several acolytes to assist. They were not undertaken lightly and the slightest mistake could have disastrous consequences. Major wards that failed outright often ended in the deaths of all involved in the casting.

Not only could wards be used to keep people away from a particular location, they could also be used to keep someone or something confined. In this case, Cade hoped to use the wards to shield Gabrielle's body from outside interference while at the same time providing him some protection should the Adversary have left any unexpected surprises.

Cade followed Clearwater up the stairs but remained in the doorway so he'd be out of her way. He watched as she wandered slowly around the twin bed, observing Gabrielle's body from every angle. Apparently satisfied with what she saw, she reached out and tried to lay her palm on Gabrielle's forehead.

Much to Cade's surprise, she was unable to do so.

She tried again, with the same result. Each time her hand would stop a few inches above Gabrielle's flesh and no matter how hard she tried, she couldn't get it to go any closer.

She stepped back, clearly puzzled. Cade was, too. Neither he nor Riley had any problem moving Gabrielle from the cemetery.

"Is there...?"

She held up a hand, stopping him in mid-sentence. Digging into the satchel at her side, she rooted around in its depths until she drew out a long-handled mirror. She made a few odd-looking gestures over it with her free hand and then exhaled heavily on its surface, fogging the glass. Before it could clear she held the mirror over Gabrielle and stared into its depths.

A grimace crossed her face.

Cade opened his mouth, intending to ask what she was doing, but the intense expression on her face made him change his mind. Instead, he waited patiently for her to finish.

After a second longer look in the mirror she put it down and turned to face him.

"Your wife isn't dead," she said.

CHAPTER 5

"ALMOST DEAD"

AVING EXPECTED HER TO COME to that conclusion, particularly after the Necromancer's comments and his own experience with the body, Cade wasn't surprised by her announcement. He focused on the practical aspect of the situation.

"How can that be?"

Clearwater sighed and sat back on her haunches. "I don't know exactly. It's as if she's stuck in that moment between life and death. Here, look."

She waited for him to join her, kneeling beside the bed, and then lifted the mirror again.

"This is a scrying mirror. Normally I use it to locate an object or person that I'm looking for, like the way a dowsing rod is used to find water. But it can also be used to view an object more clearly, to look beyond the obvious. In this case, I used it to "see" your wife's body, hoping it might show me something about the binding that you mentioned on the phone. What it showed me...well, you'd best see it for yourself."

Clearwater repeated her actions with the mirror, but this time angled it so Cade could see what it had to show.

A glimmering web of deep blue energy wrapped itself around Gabrielle an inch or so from her flesh, a literal reminder to Cade of how they had been trapped in the Adversary's web like two hapless flies. Yet that wasn't what had caught Clearwater's attention. Beneath the binding, Gabrielle's body was covered by a shadow of the deepest grey Cade had ever seen, darker even than the angry summer storm clouds he'd watched roll across the plains as a child.

"What is that?" he whispered, as if afraid of disturbing something.

Clearwater's answer was matter of fact. "Her aura. Or what's left of it actually. Her spirit, her soul if you will, has clearly left but her body still lives on in some strange fashion. It seems trapped outside the natural cycle of entropy, held in that particular moment of time, which is why we've seen no sign of decomposition or decay. She might not be breathing, but I wouldn't necessarily call her dead."

"So what does that mean? Is there anything that can be done about it?"

Clearwater shrugged. "I haven't got a clue. That one's way above my pay grade, so to speak."

The knight commander mulled it over.

"Can you still cast the wards?"

"I don't see why not. Since they affect the space around her, rather than her directly, I don't think it will be a problem."

Agreeing the wards were probably the best bet for the time being, at least until Cade understood a bit more about what he was dealing with, the two of them settled down to work. Cade helped Clearwater pull the bed away from the wall and then moved the rest of the furniture off to the side of the room, giving Clearwater plenty of space in which to work. While she disappeared downstairs to get a few things from her car, Cade took a small folding table out of the closet and set it up a few feet away from the bed, giving Clearwater a platform from which to work. When she returned she was carrying a cardboard box. She put the box on the floor and began sorting through it, occasionally taking an item and placing it on the table Cade had set up for her. It wasn't long before there was an odd assortment of items there. Cade recognized the brass thurible and the incense boat that went along with it, though he hadn't seen one outside of a Catholic Mass before. The same thing could be said for the silver chalice that she set beside them. He wasn't sure if the bottle of water was a part of the ritual or just in case she got thirsty, but he figured he'd find out soon enough. A large red candle, several long wooden matches, and a jar of what looked to be salt completed the ensemble.

Clearwater took several chunks of incense cake from inside the boat and placed it in the base of the thurible. She lit the incense with one of the matches and, picking up the thurible, moved to the head of the bed.

"Interrupting me once the casting has begun can be dangerous for both of us, so no matter what you see or hear, stay out of the circle and out of the way."

Cade indicated that he understood.

Clearwater lifted the thurible and blew in through one of the holes on the lid, fanning the burning incense so that yellow smoke began to pour forth. Satisfied with the color and density of the smoke, she turned to the east and began gently rocking the thurible back and forth on its chain.

She walked a slow circle around the bed, the incense hanging in the air as she passed, creating a ring of yellow smoke that followed in her wake and filled the room with a thick, cloying scent. When she returned to the head of the bed and the ring of incense smoke was complete, she drew the shutters on the thurible, preventing any more from coming out.

She resumed her starting position, facing away from the bed, her hands lifted to either side. "O Guardian of the East, Ancient One of the Air, I call you to attend us this night. I do summon, stir and charge you to witness our rites and guard this Circle. Send your messenger among us, so that we might know that we have your blessing, and protect us with your holy might."

A light breeze caressed Cade's cheek, stirring his hair. Within seconds the breeze strengthened to become a wind, churning the ring of smoke around the bed, spreading it out and pushing it upward until it formed a hazy yellow dome that surrounded the area Clearwater had marked out with her steps.

The smoke stung Cade's eyes and tickled his nose, as he strained to see through its depths. Through the haze he could see Clearwater still standing where she had been moments before, but now her clothes stuck to her frame as if pushed there by a gale-force wind and her long hair streamed out behind her as if held by ghostly hands. Her gaze was directed upward, over her head, and Cade couldn't help but follow her line of sight.

His mouth dropped open in surprise.

A giant bird of dark grey smoke hovered above her, stirring the air inside the circle with every powerful thrust of its great wings. Even as he watched, it turned its head toward him, its beak opening, its empty eyes piercing him to his very soul, and in the back of his mind he heard its shrieking cry of hunger and warning.

Cade glanced away, unable to meet the naked threat in its eyes, and when he looked back Clearwater was alone. The bird was gone, as was the dome of yellow incense smoke.

Clearwater turned and, catching the expression on his face, gave him a wink before moving back to the table and preparing for the second part of the ritual. She returned the thurible to its position and picked up the candle and another match. She walked around the bed until she faced the south this time and then placed the candle on the floor directly in front of her. Striking the match against the wooden floor, she lit the candle.

"O Guardian of the South, Ancient One of the Flames, I call you to attend us this night. I do summon, stir and charge you to witness our rites and guard this Circle. Send your messenger among us, so that we might know that we have your blessing, and protect us with your holy might."

No sooner had she finished speaking that the candle flame flared up like a bonfire, flooding the room with scorching heat. For just a moment Cade thought he saw a large, dragon-like creature made entirely of flames standing before Clearwater, but then the flame returned to normal and whatever it had been, if it had been there at all, was gone. The candle was once more just a candle and Clearwater stood alone.

Leaving the candle in place, she took up the chalice. She filled it with water from the bottle and moved to the end of the bed, facing Cade where he stood in the doorway. She raised the chalice in front of her and called out a third time.

"O Guardian of the West, Ancient One of the Waves, I call you to attend us this night. I do summon, stir and charge you to witness our rites and guard this Circle. Send your messenger among us, so that we might know that we have your blessing, and protect us with your holy might."

Nothing happened.

Another minute ticked passed.

Then two more.

Without warning a thunderclap roared throughout the room. No sooner had the echoes died away that rain poured from the ceiling, hammering them in a torrential downpour. Something large and wet loomed overhead, like a wave about to break over them, and in the next instant the rain stopped and Clearwater, Gabrielle, and the room around them were dry.

Cade, however, was soaked to the skin, his hair plastered against the sides of his head.

Apparently even the Guardians of the Quarters have a sense of humor.

Seeing him, Clearwater cracked a bemused smile and then went on with the ritual.

Taking the jar of salt, she moved to the bed for the final time. Facing north, she uncapped the bottle and began retracing the steps she'd taken when using the incense burner, pouring out the salt into the floor in an unbroken line as she went.

The by-now familiar incantation accompanied her. "O Guardian of the North, Ancient One of the Earth, I call you to attend us this night. I do summon, stir and charge you to witness our rites and guard this Circle. Seal this Circle with your strength and let neither man nor beast break it until the Word is given."

As she said the last, Clearwater stepped to the other side of the salt line and brought the two ends together in an unbroken circle that completely encircled the bed. When the two ends touched there was a sudden trembling in the floor beneath their feet and the line of salt changed in a heartbeat from white to a deep forest green. A new kind of tension filled the air, as if every molecule had gained an additional charge.

"Well now, that should do it," Denise said, stepping back from the circle as she replaced the lid on the jar of salt.

Cade looked at Gabrielle's unmoving body atop the bed and the line of salt that surrounded it. "That's it?" he asked, not quite sure what it was he'd been expecting but knew it certainly wasn't a line of green sand surrounding his wife's body.

Clearwater glanced at him.

"What were you expecting? A host of heavenly angels to stand guard?"

"Can you do that?" A scream of angels would be perfect. The last one he'd run into had scared the hell out of him; he had no doubt that Gabrielle's body would go unmolested with them standing watch.

Clearwater let out a sharp bark of laughter. "If you'd wanted that, you should have called Mother Church rather than a beaten-up old hedge witch."

"You're not old. And I don't want the Church involved. But come on, a line of green salt? What's that going to do if the agents of the Adversary come knocking?"

Clearwater stared at him. "You don't see it?"

Cade was baffled. Don't see what? But then it occurred to him that if he were looking for mystical effects he'd probably be much better off using something other than his ordinary eye sight to do it. Turning back to face the bed, he triggered his Sight.

A shimmering wall of emerald green energy completely encased the bed. It was so thick that Cade was unable to see through it. Neither the bed or Gabrielle's body were visible and he had no doubt that the ward would protect her from everything all the way up to an attack by one of the Fallen. Maybe even one of those, too.

"Satisfied?" Clearwater asked.

Cade deactivated his Sight and turned back in her direction. "Very. Now how do I bring it down if I need to?"

They spent the next ten minutes covering the proper ritualistic phrases that Cade could use to disband the warding and then he helped her gather her things and carry them back down to her car.

"Thanks, Denise. I owe you."

She nodded. "And don't think I won't collect on it."

They said their goodbyes and Cade watched her drive off into the night. When he could no longer see her taillights, he wandered back inside, changed into dry clothes and camped out in the room next to the bed on which his wife's not-quite-dead body lay, wondering just what the hell he was going to do next.

CHAPTER 6

"AN UNEXPECTED ARRIVAL"

THE NEXT MORNING FOUND CADE at the commandery trapped in a series of planning meetings with the other senior force commanders. He was by nature a man of few words, one who preferred to be doing things rather than sitting around talking about them, but a highly specialized organization like the Templars didn't run itself on action alone and so several times a week, when he wasn't out on a mission, he was required to sit through organizational briefings like this one. An officer from Planning and Logistics was currently at the front of the room, outlining the new method for requisitioning additional office supplies that would be put in place for the coming quarter and Cade quickly tuned him out before the man's nasal voice could set his nerves further on edge than they already were. Instead, his thoughts turned inward, pondering recent events, trying to put the pieces of the puzzle together in a way that made some kind of sense.

It didn't help that in the last few weeks his entire world had been turned on its ear.

For seven long years he'd believed that his beloved wife, Gabrielle, had escaped the pain and suffering of this world and had moved on to another, better place. He'd taken comfort in that belief, had found safety and solace in the fact that something good, something pure, had emerged from that horrific July afternoon when the supernatural entity that he called the Adversary had invaded their home and stolen her life away, that her death had not been the last and final act in the beautiful performance that had been her life.

Then had come that night seven months ago, when she'd first appeared to him in the darkness of an aircraft cabin high above the eastern seaboard, and his hard won equilibrium had been shattered like so much stained glass. She'd returned to him several times since, both here and in the Beyond, and he'd gradually begun to understand that she wasn't at rest, wasn't at rest at all, that she was trapped in some sort of limbo existence, neither here nor there, unable to return to the living and incapable of moving into the gentle peace of the dead.

It was a horrifying realization.

To think that she had been trapped in that hellish existence, alone, for all of those years, made him want to rail at the heavens and hang his head in shame. He'd failed her earlier, when he was unable to prevent the Adversary from taking her away from him, and he'd apparently failed her again, leaving her to languish in that strange half-life on the other side of the Veil.

But last night's events had been the final blow to whatever equilibrium he had managed to maintain over the years in the wake of his wife's death. The discovery of Gabrielle's body, perfectly preserved after seven years in the grave, had struck

Cade with all the delicate finesse of a sledgehammer. It made it unmistakably clear that Gabrielle was an important part of whatever plan the Adversary had set in motion, just as Cade himself was.

The question was why? What had the two of them done to deserve being targeted in such a fashion? What made them special? Out of all the billions of people in the world, why had the Adversary chosen them?

Cade's musings were interrupted by a commotion at the door. He glanced up, startled back into the present, to find Riley standing with his head just inside the entrance, gesturing to him. Excusing himself, Cade joined his senior non-com outside the door.

"Tell me you've come to rescue me," Cade said with a relieved smile on his face.

But Riley could only wearily shake his head. "We've got a problem."

* * *

The package sat opposite him, just on the other side of the gate, right in the center of the drive where it couldn't be missed. Looking down at it, Cade could see the big black letters covering the white address label, the handwriting little better than a scrawl but still legible nonetheless.

Cade Williams.

He glanced over at Riley, who said, "The guard on duty is named Samuels. Claims he was at his post in the guard house the entire time. Swears no one could have come down that road without him knowing about it, never mind leave a package right under his nose."

"Yet there it is," Cade said pointedly, looking down at the parcel. It wasn't much bigger than a hardcover book, maybe eight by twelve or so, wrapped in a plain brown paper wrapper like hundreds of other parcels a person sees over the years.

But this one was addressed to him personally.

And it had been delivered to a place that was as far as the general public was concerned nothing more than a private residence. One that was in someone else's name to boot.

Something was very wrong here.

"Does he think it just dropped out of the open sky?" Cade asked beneath his breath.

There was no answer from Riley, who either hadn't heard him or simply chose to pretend that he hadn't. Either way, Cade figured that it was probably best.

The explosives team showed up then and so he moved back a respectful distance, Riley at his side, and the two of them watched the specialists get to work.

The gates were carefully opened, giving the team access to the package, but without disturbing it in any way. A pair of dogs was then brought up, one to check for explosive residue, the other for drugs. Neither of them alerted, so the team leader ordered a pair of bomb techs to approach the package and give it a closer look.

The men were dressed in standard bomb suits that were made from an inner layer of ballistic cloth and an outer layer of fire retardant fabric and were composed of a sleeved coat and trousers, a chest plate and groin protector, and a helmet with face shield. Protective spats were also worn over the feet. The suits made them bulky and slow, but for what they were doing that was just fine. Bomb technicians who were in a hurry usually didn't live very long.

They laid a large piece of ballistic cloth, a bomb blanket, out on the ground next to the package. Checking first for an anti-lift device and not finding one, the tech used a pair of large metal tongs to gently lift the package and place it in the center of the blanket. Moving carefully, the two men then wrapped the package with the rest of the blanket. The material was designed to help contain the blast if something went wrong. That in turn went inside a heavily shielded transport crate and to Cade it seemed like everyone present breathed a sigh of relief as the door of the crate was closed.

He knew the team would take the package inside where they would first x-ray it from every possible angle before running it through a barrage of additional tests including a full chemical and biological weapons scan and then, and only then, would they attempt to open it to see what it contained.

As they watched the team move off, the crate carried carefully between them, Riley finally gave voice to what they both were thinking. "How did they know where to find you?"

Cade couldn't answer and that made him nervous, far more so than he cared to admit.

CHAPTER 7

"INVITATIONS"

W HEN THE NEWS CAME BACK that the explosive and forensic teams were finished with the package, Cade assembled Echo Team's command unit in the main hall's conference room to go over what they'd found. Along with Cade and Riley, the team consisted of two other sergeants, Nick Olsen and Sean Duncan. Olsen, a veteran who'd been with Echo for fifteen years, almost as long as Riley had, was slim and short, with curling reddish-brown hair and the type of grin that had you constantly looking over your shoulder, waiting for the practical joke. Duncan was the newest member of Echo, having joined several months earlier, just prior to the showdown with the Necromancer and the Council of Nine. He'd been in charge of the Preceptor's protective detail before having been transferred to the unit at Cade's direct request. He was younger than the other three men and his blonde hair and good looks probably could have been an asset to him in some other line of work. He was also prone to speaking his mind, regardless of the circumstances, which had brought him in conflict a few times with the way Cade ran the show, but so far he'd been a valuable asset and Cade was pleased with his impulsive decision to add Duncan to the unit.

By now the other two men had heard about the mysterious package Cade had received and so the knight commander wasted no time with preliminaries, instead moving directly into a discussion of what the investigative teams had found. Which, in truth, wasn't that much. The package had been free of dangerous substances; no explosives, no biological or chemical agents, no mystical wards or traps. It had been plain brown paper wrapped around a simple cigar box, the kind you can buy in any office supply store, both so common that tracking down their specific origins just wasn't worth the effort. The paper had not held any fingerprints, nor was there any trace evidence such as hair or fiber samples recovered from it. Since it had apparently been delivered by hand, there were no stamps or postmarks that could be used to try and pinpoint where it had come from either. Even the handwriting spelling out Cade's name on the front of the wrapper turned out not to be handwriting at all, but a computer based font that only looked like handwritten script. It was as clean a dead end as Cade had ever seen in all his years in law enforcement.

Which made the two items the box contained all the more interesting.

The first was a hand-written note on plain white paper, addressed to Cade.

Dear Captain Williams,

Please come quickly. Information has come into my hands that I dare not entrust to anyone else. An old foe has returned and already I fear for my safety and the safety of those around me. Time is of the essence. I will explain further when you arrive.

In Christ,
Father Thomas Martin, S.J.

The second item was a standard 4x6 snapshot of a crowd gathered in front of a church. The lab had confirmed that ordinary Kodak film had been used in processing the picture, the kind available in hundreds of thousands of drug and grocery stores across the country. The shot appeared to have been taken from a moving vehicle, for many of the faces of those gathered were slightly blurred. There was writing on the back of the photo, in the same script as the letter.

Perhaps this will help you see the urgency of my request.

The evidence team had cleared the items for handling so Cade passed them around, letting each member take a good, long look. None of them knew what to make of the photo. It seemed completely ordinary. There were ten, maybe twelve people walking down the street with the church just barely visible in the background. Most of them were looking the other way, though a few had been caught in profile. Due to the quality of the picture, none of them were identifiable, however.

Duncan asked the obvious question. "Who's Father Martin?

And why does he refer to you as Captain Williams?"

"Because the last time I saw him, I was a Captain," Cade said absently, still staring at the photo and trying to discern the meaning of Martin's cryptic comment.

Riley took pity on Duncan and tried to bring him up to speed when he saw that Cade was too preoccupied to do so. "We met Father Martin several years ago, shortly after Cade had taken command of Echo. As Cade said, he was just a lowly Captain back then," he said, earning him an amused glance from the knight commander. "Martin and several other priests in the Boston archdiocese nearby were having trouble with a new cult that had sprung up among the street gangs in the area. They contacted the Order and, since the cult had shown no hesitation to use violence against the Church, a combat squad was sent in to deal with it."

Duncan shrugged. "Sounds fairly routine."

"Yeah, you'd think so. Unfortunately, we were way off base."

"What happened?"

"The squad disappeared without a trace three weeks after arriving in the area. Eight highly trained men. Every single one of them a veteran combat soldier, trained specifically for situations like this. So of course Echo gets the call. Our orders were to find out what happened to the squad and to deal with the cult that had gotten the Order involved in the first place."

Olsen cut in. "Recognizing that the Order's initial show of force had done little good, Cade decided to take a different approach. He sent one of our men, a lieutenant, into the neighborhood undercover with orders to set up a safe house and then to make contact with the local clergy. For the first few days, everything went without a hitch. Bishop, Jonathan Bishop, that was the lieutenant's name, got us a secure location, rendezvoused with the locals, and let us know that it was okay to bring in the rest of the team. But by the time we had arrived, Bishop had vanished, just like the men from First Squad."

Olsen stared off into space as he continued and from the look on his face Duncan knew he was reliving it in his mind's eye. "We got a lead that both Bishop and the leaders of the cult could be found in an abandoned warehouse over in Roxbury. Timing was critical. First Squad was guarding the Bishop's residence in Cambridge and Second Squad was enroute. We knew we couldn't wait, so Cade made the decision to hit the warehouse with only the command squad, hoping things wouldn't get too hairy before the reinforcements arrived."

"Good Lord," Duncan said, stealing a glance across the room at Cade. "Just the three of you?"

The question brought Olsen back to the here and now. "Just the three of us. Me, Cade, and Riley. What can I say? We were younger then, younger and full of confidence. You know how it is. Sometimes you just think you're invincible."

Riley picked up the story again. "We snuck in through the skylight and from the second floor walkway we could see Bishop tied to a post in the middle of the warehouse. He wasn't moving, and with the place looking empty, we thought maybe we were too late. That they'd already executed him and left his body for us to find."

"So what did you do?"

"We made our way down to the first floor and over to where they'd left Bishop. Olsen and me, we stood watch while Cade checked him out. Turned out we were right. Bishop was cold as ice."

Riley shook his head. "That was our first mistake."

"And it was a big one," said Olsen, anger in his eyes at the memory. "Bishop might have been dead but that didn't mean he was out of the fight. We found that out the hard way when he reared up and tried to rip Cade's throat open. Course by then Riley and I had our hands full as a horde of Chiang Shih began pouring out of nowhere, charging right for us."

"Chiang what?"

"Shih. Chiang Shih. Also known as the Shadow People. As far as anyone knows they originated in China, but they've spread over the last few centuries and now can be found throughout Central and Southeast Asia. Tradition says they are formed when an individual has an outstanding karmic debt that must be paid, a debt so enormous that it prevents the soul from moving onward through the Great Cycle and forces the body to rise again from death. More often than not, the higher, rational aspect of the soul, the Hun, becomes dormant, leaving the P'o, or the lower bestial aspect of the soul, in control of the resurrected creature."

Duncan grimaced. "Sounds pleasant."

"Neither truly living nor altogether dead, the Chiang Shih are creatures without the essence of life, or Chi as the Chinese call it, and therefore must constantly steal it from the living to sustain their existence. They also have the option of turning their victims into a lesser version of themselves, blood-thirsty undead creatures that crave the flesh rather than the life force of the living."

"Which is just what we were facing," Riley cut in.

"Right. And good thing, too, as full-blood Chiang Shih aren't as susceptible to firearms as are their lesser counterparts. Cade dealt with Bishop while Riley and I held off several attacks by the others. By the time we'd beaten back the third wave, we'd run out of ammunition and had to resort to using our blades."

Duncan could see it all in his head, the three combat veterans standing back to back, the bodies of their foes littering the floor at their feet. What he couldn't understand was how they managed to survive if they were so badly outnumbered, so he asked them.

"We almost didn't," answered Olsen. "We got lucky, that's all. Second Squad showed up at the last moment, cutting into the Chiang Shih from behind, making them believe that we'd set a trap for them. Believing they were vastly outnumbered, they retreated, leaving us to clean up the mess, which wasn't that hard since the bodies turned to ash the minute their Queen disappeared out the back door."

"And Bishop? Did you ever find out what happened to him?"

Olsen and Riley shared a glance.

"Yeah," Olsen replied. "Yeah, we did."

But he didn't say anything more and before Duncan could ask him to explain further, Cade tossed the photo onto the table top in front of them, a frown of disgust plain on his face.

"I don't get it. What does he expect us to see in this thing?"

"Why don't we just call him and ask," Olsen suggested.

With the others looking on, Cade summoned an initiate and gave instructions for him to bring them any and all telephone numbers for either Father Thomas Martin or the Church of the Blessed Sorrow, both in Brookline, Massachusetts. It didn't take the initiate long to come back with the information; most of it was readily available through directory assistance and the single number that wasn't, the priest's personal cell phone, was in one of the Order's databanks.

Cade spent the next several minutes trying each number, all without success. In light of the nature of Martin's message, the lack of response made Cade more than a little uneasy and so he made a snap decision based more on instinct than reason.

"I think it's time we take a little road trip. Grab a kit bag and meet me in the motor pool in twenty."

Just like that, Echo's command unit was headed for Boston.

CHAPTER 8

"BEANTOWN"

NAGGED BY HIS INABILITY TO understand whatever it was Father Martin expected him to learn from the photograph, Cade left the manor house behind, crossed the commandery grounds on foot, and entered the science building. Photo reconnaissance was on the second floor and upon arriving, Cade asked to speak to Jarvis.

Though only twenty-five, Jarvis' skills were miles above the other members of the unit and Cade preferred the use of his services whenever possible. He explained the situation to the photo tech and asked if Jarvis could sharpen up the picture enough for them to recognize the individuals in the photo.

"Bloody piece of cake, chap," Jarvis said, beaming. "When did ya want it?"

"Yesterday."

"Got ten minutes?"

Cade glanced at his watch and then nodded. "But no more

than that."

Jarvis led him over to a computer workstation where he fed the photo into a nearby scanner. Once the picture had been digitized, he went to work.

"Every photograph is composed of millions of little dots, known as pixels. The computer analyzes the entire image and then begins to work at it one pixel at a time. Using a complex series of algorithms, it attempts to identify the most likely arrangement for each individual pixel based on the hundreds that surround it. By doing so, we can gradually clean up the image, correcting the focus, the color, even the perspective if necessary."

There were eleven individuals in all, six women and five men, and as Cade watched their faces slowly began to grow clearer. One by one he eliminated all of the women and four of the men, either because he didn't recognize them or because there was no reason to consider them a threat.

The fifth, and final, man was a different story.

The man stood with his face partially turned to the camera, a smile playing at the corners of his mouth. Judging from the other people around him, he was tall and well-built, with dirty blonde hair that came down just past the collar of the light coat he wore.

Seeing his face, Cade understood exactly what Father Martin had been trying to tell him.

The man in the photograph was his old teammate, Bishop.

* * *

The others were ready and waiting when Cade arrived at the motor pool fifteen minutes later. He explained what he'd done and then passed a copy of the enhanced image to each of them.

"Sweet Mary and Joseph!" Riley exclaimed upon seeing Bishop.

Olsen let out a low whistle of his own. "That throws a wrench into the works now, doesn't it?"

He was right; Bishop's presence in Boston changed things considerably. Cade was already thinking of the mission as a rescue operation now, rather than a fact-finding mission. Father Martin had been involved in the ill-fated operation from several years ago. He'd met Bishop when the Templar advance man had first arrived in the city and knew what had later happened to him at the hands of the Chiang Shih. He'd recognized that Bishop's presence outside his church did not bode well for the congregation, or for Martin himself, and might even signal the return of the Shadows to the city proper.

It also explained why Martin had sent a note to Cade rather than bringing in the usual authorities. The police could do little against one of the shadows. Bringing in the local authorities would only end with innocent people dead. Rather than do that, Martin reached out to those who'd saved him once before; the secret, militant arm of the Mother Church.

Cade felt a growing sense of urgency settle over him.

They climbed into the SUV assigned to them and got underway. Riley drove, with Cade riding shotgun and Olsen and Riley in the back seat. The rear of the truck was packed with a variety of gear bags and hidden in the secret compartment beneath them, the team's firearms.

They made good time, straight up 95 into the suburbs of the city, where they switched over to Route 93 that took them into the city proper. Once there, they got off highway and cruised into the streets of South Boston.

A predominantly Irish, blue collar neighborhood, South

Boston was as well known for its St. Patrick's Day celebrations as it was for its high crime rate. The Irish mob had ruled the streets for so long that even when their leadership crumbled in the face of multiple FBI investigations in the mid-90s very little had changed for the people on the streets. Life went on, just as it always had, and eventually someone else stepped up and to take the reigns of power, just as they always had and always would.

Cade had patrolled the area as a young beat cop. This was when he'd first come to know Father Martin. Cade had answered more than his share of operation calls in the neighborhood during his time on the Special Tactics and Operations Team, or STOP. He'd been back once or twice during his years with the Order, but little ever changed in Southie and it felt like only yesterday that he'd left.

As they neared the church, they could see a squad car parked in the driveway of the rectory.

"Keep going past the church and park farther down the street," Cade said and Riley obeyed. As they drove past Cade could see a uniformed officer sitting in the front seat of the squad car and the telltale yellow crime scene tape stretched across the front door of the rectory confirmed his worst suspicions.

It appeared they were too late.

Riley found an open spot a few blocks away, pulled in and turned the engine off.

"Now what?" he asked.

Cade gave it some thought. Having the four of them suddenly appear on the rectory doorstep was a bad idea, particularly if something untoward had happened to Father Martin. Cade decided to take Duncan and walk back past the church to see if they could get the uniform to tell them anything useful.

The two of them got out of the car, turning their collars up against the chill breeze, and headed off in the direction of the church. They hadn't gone half a block before Cade caught sight of a foursome moving down the street toward them, three men and a woman, and he pointed them out to Duncan. The men were dressed in the black pants and shirts of the clergy and the woman wore the deep blue habit of a Catholic nun.

"Let's see if we can get a bit of information," he said.

As they got closer, Cade stepped out and raised his hand in greeting. "Excuse me? Father?"

"Yes?" As he responded to Cade, the older of the two men stepped out in front of the other three, as if getting ready to protect them, and Cade noted how all four immediately tensed at his approach. *Easy or you'll spook them*, he thought.

"I was hoping you could help me. I'm looking for Father Martin. Can you tell me if he's still assigned to this parish?"

The nun, a young woman who couldn't have been older than her mid-twenties, raised a hand to cover her mouth and Cade felt the level of tension among the group go up dramatically.

The priest's eyes narrowed as he looked at Cade. "And what would you be wanting with Father Martin?" he asked, the hint of an accent creeping into his voice as a result of the stress.

Cade tried to look as non-threatening as possible. "It's been a few years, but Father Tom officiated at my wedding. I was back in town on business and thought I'd stop by and say hello." Cade pointed back up the street. "But the police car in the driveway made me think this might not be the best time to drop in for a visit. Has something happened?"

The group relaxed and the senior priest finally extended a hand. "I'm Father O"Malley, son, from St. Judes, a few streets over."

"Jake Caruso," Cade said, without hesitation, and then

introduced Duncan as his friend, Michael Simpson.

"I'm afraid I've got some bad news, Jake. Father Tom passed away last night."

Cade did his best to look shocked, all the while inwardly cursing this confirmation of his suspicions. "What happened?"

The younger of the three men spoke up. "Some street punk broke in and…"

O'Malley held up a hand, silencing the other. "Watch your tongue, Phillip. What will Sister Margaret think of such language?"

"Sister Margaret happens to agree with him," the young nun answered, much to both Cade and Duncan's surprise. "And I know you do, too. So tell the man what he needs to know and let's all get out of this cold."

O'Malley sighed, and Cade could hear the unspoken apology in the expression. O'Malley was clearly old school and he apparently felt Cade was cut from the same cloth.

"I'm sorry to have to tell you that Father Tom was killed last night during a burglary. Police say he must have surprised the intruder in the midst of the crime and the man panicked, resulting in Father Tom's death."

The younger priest cut in again. "He stabbed him with a butcher knife eight times and then left him to bleed to death on the kitchen floor. I hope he rots in hell." His voice cracked and Cade saw the suggestion of tears in his eyes before the man turned away. Sister Margaret put her arms around him and talked to him in a voice too low for Cade to hear.

"Do the police have any idea who did it?" Cade asked.

O'Malley shook his head. "Not yet, but I'm confident that Detective Burke will find the culprit before long."

"Detective Joseph Burke?"

O'Malley seemed surprised. "Yes, that's the one. Do you know him?"

"Another old friend from the neighborhood. I guess we never really stray far from our roots, do we, Father?"

The priest nodded. "That's true, Mr. Caruso, very true."

They spent a few more minutes talking and then Cade thanked them for their time and let them continue on their way. He waited until they had moved out of sight before walking back to the truck with Duncan and letting the others know what they'd discovered.

"So you know this guy, Burke?" Riley asked.

Cade nodded. "He worked Bunko when I was with Homicide. We did a few task forces together. Decent guy overall. Takes the job a bit too lightly for my taste, but he was never a bad cop."

Olsen spoke up from the back seat. "Think he'll help us?"

"Only one way to find out," Cade replied.

He took out his cell phone and dialed a number.

"Detective Burke, please" he said to the woman who answered.

CHAPTER 9

"FOR OLD TIMES' SAKE"

ADE STEPPED INSIDE THE DINER and looked around. Burke, a heavy set man with a close-cropped shock of white hair that always made Cade think of the white apes of Barsoom, waved to him from a seat in the back corner. Cade threaded his way through the other diners and slid into the booth opposite. The two men shook hands.

"Good to see ya, Williams. How are the Feds treating ya these days?"

Shortly after Cade had left the force, Burke had come under the mistaken impression that Cade worked for a super secret arm of the federal government, the NSA or the DIA, something along those lines, and Cade had never disabused him of the notion. It had been helpful to have someone on the inside over the years and right now, Burke was their best chance of getting a line on what was going on.

"Good as can be expected, I guess," Cade answered, as he

signaled the waitress for a cup of coffee. "Thanks for meeting me."

"No problem." He waited until the waitress had brought Cade's coffee, refilled Burke's own, and walked over to take care of another customer at a different table before continuing. "You here about that priest down in Southie?"

"Yeah. Word on the street says it was a burglary gone sideways?"

Burke nodded. "Damnedest thing, too. I mean, the guy was old, right? All the perp had to do was push him out of the way. Instead he grabs a butcher knife from the block in the kitchen and stabs the guy to death." The detective took a sip of his coffee. "Professional interest?" he asked.

"Nah. Personal. I knew Father Martin from back in the day. Used to see him at church when I was a kid. He came to see me at the Deaconess a few times, during my recovery."

He knew he didn't have to explain just what he was recovering from; for a cop who'd known him as long as Burke had, there could be only one incident he was referring to, the assault on Cade and his wife by the Dorchester Demon seven years ago. "Last I'd heard he'd retired."

Burke nodded. "Retired from the hospital, but not from active ministry. He went back to working as the assistant pastor at St. John the Divine, back where he started all those years ago." He picked up a dark folder from the seat beside him, looked at it without speaking for a moment, and then seemed to come to a decision. He passed the folder to Cade. "Figured this was what you were calling about, so I brought the file."

Cade opened the folder and a deep sense of trepidation unfolded in his gut. He hadn't known Thomas well, but the man had been kind to him in a time when kindness was more precious than life itself and so he'd always had a soft place in his heart for the tough old soldier of Christ. Inside were several 8.5 x 11 full-color photos. The first showed Martin where he had fallen on the floor of rectory kitchen, his blood staining the cracked linoleum and his face turned toward the camera as if his unseeing eyes were staring deep into the lens. The black handle of a carving knife protruded from his back. The second was a closer view of Father Martin's back, showing several slashes in the fabric of his shirt, evidence of other entrance wounds. Cade counted ten without even trying.

The other photos showed the body from various angles, but didn't give him anything new.

"Any witnesses?"

Burke shook his head. "The rectory houses two other priests, but both were away at an archdiocesan conference and the housekeeper had the weekend off. She was the one who found him when she came in this morning."

"How about trace evidence?"

"I'm still waiting for a few tests to come back from forensics, but as of right now we've got nothing. The knife, doorknobs, and sink were all wiped clean. Hair and fiber came up empty as well. I'm having the blood splatters typed, hoping we get lucky, but I'm really not counting on it. Whoever the guy was, he played it cool and seems to have gotten away without leaving anything behind."

Cade knew there was more to it than that, but he couldn't say so to Burke. If Bishop were involved, as Cade suspected, things might just get a lot uglier.

"That just sucks. What did the thief make off with? A couple of gold-plated chalices and the money from the poor box?"

"Not even. Idiot dropped his sack when he turned to run.

Damned shame is what it is."

They spent another fifteen minutes sharing war stories and catching up on guys they knew. When they ran out of things to talk about, Cade thanked Burke for coming down and paid the bill.

As Burke got up to go, Cade reached out and grabbed his arm.

"Where did they take Martin's body?"

"The County Morgue was full so they've got him over at the Annex, in the basement of Mass General. Gonna go pay your respects?"

Cade glanced away.

"Yeah." *Something like that.*

CHAPTER 10

"MESSAGES IN THE DARK"

C ADE DIDN'T HAVE THE LUXURY to take things slowly at this point. He needed a look at Father Martin's body and he needed to do it now. The fact that it was being housed over at the morgue annex, rather than the primary facility at Boston City Hall was a definite plus. Foot traffic was much lower at the Annex and he knew they should be able to get in and out without too much difficulty. More importantly, the chances of someone from his past recognizing him at the Annex were much lower than they would be at City Hall.

Cade waited five minutes after Burke had left and then returned to the vehicle. A few minutes later Riley opened the passenger door and climbed in beside him.

"Well?" Cade asked.

"Went straight back to his car and drove off. I took down the tags but I don't think there's anything for us to worry about. He didn't have a tail and I don't see any evidence of a stakeout; the rest of the cars along the street are empty. There wasn't any activity in the windows of the building overlooking the diner, either."

"Good." He'd thought Burke was playing on the up and up, but it didn't hurt to be sure. Cade sat there in silence for a moment and then made up his mind. He needed a look at that body and there was no better time than the present.

"Get a hold of the other two and let them know we're headed over to the morgue. We'll meet up with them back at the hotel once we're finished."

"Roger that."

While Riley was on the phone, Cade opened the storage compartment between the front seats. He pressed a hidden stud and then lifted the compartment out entirely, revealing another, shallower space beneath. He removed several leather identification cases from inside the hollow and flipped through them. Selecting two, he replaced the rest and then reseated the upper compartment.

He waited until Riley had hung up and then handed over one of the sets of ID.

"Who are we this time?" asked the sergeant.

"NSA."

"Works for me."

Cade knew the average municipal employee wouldn't ask too many questions of a representative of the National Security Agency, the arm of the US government responsible for the collection and analysis of foreign communications, and so it seemed like a good choice. Believed by some to be the world's largest intelligence-gathering agency, the NSA was a branch of the Department of Defense and with that affiliation came a certain sense that the less one knew about its activities the better.

Cade was counting on that reputation of secrecy to allow them to get in and out of the morgue without having to explain what they were doing there.

He knew he could have simply asked Burke for access to the body, but that would have resulted in a paper trail. Right now his meeting with Burke was off the books and Cade intended to keep things that way.

They made the short trip downtown and parked across the street from the Annex to avoid the cameras that Cade knew where set up around the government parking lot adjacent to the building. They showed their credentials to the guard just inside the front door and then took the elevator down to the basement where they let the morgue attendant know what they wanted.

The attendant led them over to the bank of steel drawers built into the far wall and pulled one of them open, exposing the black body bag that lay inside. He deftly slid the bag onto a portable table, wheeled the table over to one of the examinations stations, and then repeated the process in reverse. Once the bag was in place, the attendant unzipped the thick plastic, exposing the body of an elderly man. He checked the toe tag against the clipboard he carried and then removed a file from a nearby cabinet, handing it to Cade.

"That's him," he said, indicating the body, "and that's the autopsy report. Just what are you looking for?"

Cade took the clipboard, smiled at the attendant, and said, "Thanks. Now if you wouldn't mind waiting in the hall?"

The attendant smiled back. "Sorry, no can do. Rules say I've got to be here."

"Riley?"

"Yes, sir." The big man stepped up, took the attendant by the arm and led him toward the door. "I'm sorry, sir," he said, speaking over the man's protests, "but this is a matter of national security. You are going to have to wait in the hall until we're finished."

"National security? What the hell does the death of a priest have to do with national security?"

"Sorry, sir, but I can't tell you that. Your government appreciates your assistance in this matter, however, and I'm sure that…"

Riley's voice faded as he escorted the man out into the hallway. Moments later he stepped back inside the room and then shut and locked the door behind him. He took up a stance in front of it, just to be certain they wouldn't be interrupted.

Satisfied, Cade turned back to the autopsy report in his hands. He leafed through it for a few moments, noting the time of death as having been between late last night and early this morning. The pieces seemed to fit together. He could see Martin making the drive to Connecticut, dropping off the package, and the returning early that morning only to find the intruder in the midst of the burglary. Surprised, the thief reacts without thinking and suddenly he's got a murder rap to add to his breaking and entering and burglary charges.

Cause of death was listed as exsanguination, caused by multiple knife wounds to the chest. Father Martin had bled to death alone there in the early morning darkness, unable to call for help. Cade found himself hoping the old man hadn't suffered too much, that his faith had allowed him to face death with the same bravery and determination with which he'd faced life.

The report noted that the wounds were caused by a common kitchen knife, that the weapon had been recovered at the scene, and that the nature of the wounds matched the size and shape of the blade. The knife itself had been sent to the lab for analysis, so Cade was not going to be able to examine it for himself.

But he had the next best thing.

Martin's body.

He put the report down and turned to Riley. "M.E. puts his death sometime last night, early this morning, which means we've still got time to give this a shot."

"I'm ready when you are."

"All right. You know what to do if anything goes wrong."

Knowing he was in good hands, Cade turned back to the body and took a few deep breaths, preparing himself mentally for what was to come, and then removed the thin cotton gloves that he habitually wore, the gloves that kept him functional and sane.

Seven years before, back when Cade worked for the Boston police department, he'd come face to face with a supernatural entity he'd come to know as the Adversary. That encounter had scarred his body and his soul, and had left him with a few unique abilities. He was about to use one of them now.

Cade called it his Gift, though for years he had considered it more a curse than a benefit. Still, there was no denying its usefulness at times like this. By touching an object with his bare hands, Cade could read the psychic impressions that had been left on it by the last person to handle it. Thoughts and feelings poured out in his head as if he were actually experiencing them. They didn't last long, a few seconds at most, and the impressions faded from the object over time so that after forty-eight hours or so he was unable to get anything worthwhile from them. But if he got to the object in time, he could learn a tremendous amount of useful information.

If he used his Gift on the deceased, he could "experience" their last moments just as they had. If Martin had gotten a glimpse of his attacker, Cade would see the same thing. In addition, he'd have access to whatever Martin was thinking at the time, allowing for an even greater understanding.

The technique wasn't without its dangers, however, for Cade not only saw what the deceased had seen, but experienced it as well. If the priest had been scared, Cade would be scared. If the priest had been injured, Cade would feel his pain; his body would react as if he himself had been injured. Occasionally the wounds themselves would manifest on his body, which made every use of his Gift a potentially deadly one.

Riley would be his backup. If it looked like Cade was in trouble, he would break the connection by pulling Cade away from the body. That was usually enough to prevent further harm, though occasionally more forceful measures were required. Cade hoped today wouldn't be one of those times.

With a final nod to Riley, Cade reached out and touched Father Martin's face.

Darkness.

The sense of being followed, no, hunted, as he scrambled up a long incline, the rocks sharp against the flesh of his hands.

Had to warn them.

Had to warn them all before it was too late!

His breath came hard and heavy, his ankle hurt where he'd twisted it earlier, but he dared not stop. If he did, they'd kill him. There was no question in his mind.

A strange baying sound reached his ears and his heart leapt into his throat. It wouldn't be long now; they'd released the hounds.

Darkness.

Inside the church.

The feel of the holy wafer on his tongue.

Figures moving in the darkness around him, holding his arms out to the sides, the altar steps hard against his knees, but he had eyes only for the crucifix on the wall above the altar before him.

Pain ripped through his body, but he did all he could to ignore it, focusing on the message he had to pass on.

The cross, Captain.

You must find the cross!

The image of a red, Templar cross swam before his eyes and he concentrated on it, fighting the pain, holding out as long as he could, the cross centered before him.

Someone moved to stand in front of him and a new, savage pain ripped through his body, forcing him to lose his concentration, his eyes focusing on the man standing before him, the blond haired man who leaned forward into the light so that he could get a good look at his face as he slammed the knife into his chest...

Riley hauled Cade away from the body of the priest, turning him away just as the other man vomited up a great gout of blood that splashed on the floor tiles at their feet as if it had been poured from a bucket high above their heads, blood from a wound that didn't even exist. Cade coughed several more times, clearing his throat, spitting up the last of the blood that had filled his mouth in the same way that it had filled Martin's, a result of the knife that had been driven into his chest by the man standing before him.

A man Cade recognized.

Bishop.

When he could speak, he told Riley everything that he had seen, including the identity of Martin's killer. They had the confirmation they needed. Bishop was back and he was up to no good.

But Martin had left them a clue, a clue meant specifically for the Order, and if they could find it they might understand just what was going on.

CHAPTER 11

"HONOR AMONG THIEVES"

THE BAR WAS A DIVE joint named Maxine's. It stood on the corner of Sunset and Main, not too far from Mattapan Square. It wasn't one of Burke's usual hangouts; in fact, he rarely came to Mattapan, which was precisely why he chose the place. The chances anyone would recognize him were slim to none and he could get his business done and get out of there before anyone was the wiser.

He could only find a spot a few blocks away, which ticked him off but what were you going to do? It wasn't like he could park out front with his police placard on the dash. His car wouldn't last ten minutes in this neighborhood. Grabbing his handheld off the seat beside him, he turned up his collar, walked up the street, and entered the bar.

Once his eyes adjusted to the dim lighting, he could see that his business partner was waiting for him in the last booth. He made his way through the crowd but rather than slide into the booth across from the other man, where he'd have his back to the door, he pulled a chair from a nearby table and sat in the aisle at the head of the table.

The man he'd come to see grinned slyly as Burke settled down and the detective knew the set-up had been intentional. *Probably trying to piss me off, put me off my game.* He gave the other man his best Fuck You smile in return, just to show he wouldn't be so easily rattled.

He signaled the waitress for a beer, waited until she brought it, and then spent another minute watching her ass as she walked off again. When he felt he'd made his point, he turned back to the other man and said, "It's done. He took the bait."

A smile spread across the face of the man opposite and that simple gesture accomplished what the gamesmanship before could not; Burke suddenly felt incredibly uncomfortable. The urge to get the hell out of there was practically overwhelming and he went so far as to slide his chair back slightly before his rational mind regained control. *Chill out, stupid,* he thought. *You aint' got what you came here for yet.*

"And the patrol car?"

Burke grunted. "I'll make the call as soon as I'm out of here."

The blonde haired man shook his head. "Make it now, please."

It was far more an order than a request, but in that moment he decided to just do what needed to be done, get his money, and then get the hell out of there, before things got out of hand.

The detective removed a handheld radio from his pocket, checked the frequency and then pushed the talk button.

"Grearson? This is Burke."

He waited a moment and then repeated the call.

Burke was about to do it a third time when the radio crackled and the other man's voice came back through it. "Grearson here, Detective. Sorry about that; had to take a piss."

Burke bit his tongue, forcing back the caustic comment that sprang to mind. Just get it done, he thought. Get it done and wash your hands of all of this.

"We've got the eyes set up in the building across the street, so you can return to regular patrol. Thanks for your help."

"Ten four, Detective. Thanks for the overtime."

"Roger that, Grearson. Burke out."

The detective turned the radio off and returned it to the pocket of his coat. Returning his attention to the other man, he said, "I've pulled the black and white off the site. They shouldn't have any trouble getting inside the church now."

"Very good. I believe that completes our arrangement then."

Burke sneered. "Not quite. There's still the matter of my pay."

Blondie chuckled. "Ah yes, your thirty pieces of silver." He took a small gym bag off the seat next to him and shoved it across the table at Burke.

The bag was unzipped so the detective pulled the flaps open and peered inside. The bag was full of bundles of cash, 100s wrapped in red rubber bands as if fresh from the mint. Burke reached inside, picked a random bundle from deeper in the bag and, without lifting it above the confines of the bag itself, flipped through it, making certain that they were all bills and not stacks of paper wrapped in loose cash.

Satisfied with what he saw, he stood, zipped the bag, and addressed his companion.

"Looks like our business is done. If I see you in my district again, I'll arrest you on sight, understand?"

Blondie didn't say anything, just grinned that unsettling

smile, and Burke decided it was time to get out of there. He grabbed the bag, made his way back through the crowd and headed down the street toward his car.

He was almost there when the voice came out of the darkness.

"Whooo-wee! Lookey what we got here, boys. What you doing in this neighborhood after dark whitey?"

Several dark forms stepped out of the alley in front of him, blocking his way.

Burke stared disdainfully at the youths. There were five of them, maybe six, not a one older than their late teens. All of them were black, which explained the racial comment.

Damned punks.

Out loud, he said, "I'm a cop and unless all of you want to spend the night in lockup being somebody's bubba, I suggest you get the fuck out of my way."

No one moved.

"Oh for fuck's sake," Burke said and drew his firearm, pointing it at the group's leader. Now he was pissed. First that idiot in the bar and now these punks? Doesn't anybody remember how to show their betters the respect they deserve? He'd had enough. "Back off or I'll blow your stupid heads off!" he said.

The only answer was the sharp sound of the slides on several handguns being jacked back.

Oh shit, Burke had time to think, and then everything went to hell.

The detective managed to get off the first two shots. He wasn't all that bad with a firearm, either, putting the leader down with a double tap to the head before the other man could even squeeze the trigger.

But it was five to one and the street punks knew what it was that Burke was carrying in that leather bag he held in his left hand and wanted it, wanted it all, and if some of their number got hurt in the bargain, well then, they'd just have to live with that. More dough for the survivors. With that kind of dough they could set themselves up for a long time to come…

The end was never in doubt, though Burke did manage to take three of them with him before he succumbed to his wounds and collapsed onto the street. He'd been hit, eight, maybe ten times, and he knew he had only seconds to live. Already his arms and legs were going numb, his vision starting to grey out around the edges.

The survivors hauled the bag out of his grasp and he dimly heard the slap of their sneakers against the pavement as they raced away into the darkness, leaving him lying there alone, bleeding out.

Wait, not alone, he thought, as someone stepped out of the dark mouth of the alley to his left.

Help, he tried to say, but all that came out was a thin gurgle and a mouthful of fresh blood. He turned his head, letting the blood dribble out onto the street beneath him, and when he turned it back again he found Blondie standing over him.

"Don't you read your Bible, Burke? Judas doesn't escape his fate."

There was that smile again and then the blonde haired man dropped to the pavement atop him and Burke knew no more.

CHAPTER 12

"GATEWAY"

A FTER LEAVING THE MORGUE ANNEX, Cade and Riley rejoined the other two men at the hotel room they'd checked into a few blocks from the church. Cade filled them in with what they had discovered.

"So now what?" asked Duncan.

"Martin left something in the church for us to find. We've got to find a way to get inside and take a look around, without the police hanging around."

"That's not going to be easy," Riley said and Cade agreed. They just didn't have any choice. They had to get inside that church.

As it turned out, things were far easier than any of them expected. On their first drive-by, they discovered the patrol car had been taken off the rectory and subsequent passes didn't reveal the telltale presence of a police stake-out anywhere around the property.

The foursome parked a few blocks away and then made their way back up the street in pairs, passing between the rectory and the church to reach the rear entrance. Olsen pulled out his lock picks and got to work. It took him less than a minute to breach the structure and they were inside with, they hoped, no one the wiser.

From there, they quickly got to work.

* * *

"It has to be here somewhere!"

They'd been searching for two hours and still hadn't found anything remotely resembling the red Templar cross that Cade had seen in his vision. They'd examined the pews, looking to see if the symbol had been carved into the surface. They'd searched each and every panel of the stained glass windows, wrongly assuming that something so bright would be hidden among things that were equally so. There, too, they'd come up empty, however. Riley had even used a set of binoculars to get a close look at the entire ceiling and still they'd had nothing.

Now they sat together at the edge of the altar platform, trying to decide on their next move. None of them doubted that there was something here to find. Cade's visions had never been wrong. But sometimes they had been more than a touch ambiguous and this certainly seemed to qualify as one of those times. Each of them were as frustrated as Cade was at this point.

"Maybe we're being too literal."

Cade turned to look at him. "What do you mean?"

Olsen frowned, searching for the words to say what he meant. "It's like this. Martin obviously knew someone was after him. Might have even known that they were aware of you and possibly the Order as well, right?"

"Right. Tell me something I don't know."

"Well, then, think about it. Put yourself in Martin's shoes. If you knew someone was after you, knew that you had vital information that had to be passed on regardless of what happened to you personally, would you have left something in plain sight for anyone to find? Especially a symbol that the enemy might recognize?"

Cade frowned. "Of course not."

"But that's what we've been looking for," said Olsen. "We are assuming that the cross you saw was something Martin was looking at in the final moments of his life, but what if that's not the case? What if he were simply focused on the Order itself? What if his hope for rescue simply translated into a mental image of the symbol of his rescuers?"

Cade had to admit it was possible, but in this case, unlikely. He couldn't prove it, but he'd had the distinct sense that Martin had been trying to pass him a message and whatever that message was, it was linked to a red cross.

He glanced around the interior of the church, trying not to focus on anything in particular. Maybe Olsen was right; maybe they were being too literal.

His gaze took in the rows of pews before him and then moved on to the organ player's booth above them. He pivoted when he sat, turned his attention to the altar itself. He stared hard at the crucifix hanging on the wall behind it, let his gaze wander over the cloth-covered tabernacle in the rear corner, moved on to the lectern, then the plaque representing one of the Stations of the Cross on the wall nearby...

Wait.

He turned back.

Something about the tabernacle...

Then he had it. The tabernacle was a symbol of the Holy of Holies, the sacred chamber at the heart of King Solomon's Temple. It was accessible only once a year and then only by the High Priest, for it was the place where God himself resided.

Similarly, the Knights Templar hadn't always been known as such. Once, long ago, the Order had been called another, more formal name.

The Poor Knights of Christ of the Temple of Solomon.

The Temple, or the modern day version, the tabernacle, was the place where the Church and the Order intersected.

That had to be it!

Cade jumped to his feet, startling the others. He crossed the room and pulled back the cloth that covered the tabernacle. There, in the very center of the small gold door that allowed access to the storage space inside, was a keyhole outlined in red.

A keyhole in the shape of a Templar cross.

"Good for you, old man," Cade whispered.

The small "door" to the tabernacle was locked but that was only a minor deterrent to Cade. Now was not the time for niceties, he knew. He drew his combat knife from the sheath in his boot and was preparing to wedge the door open when Olsen interrupted.

"What are you going to do with that?" he asked.

"What's it look like?" Cade replied. "I'm going to open the door."

"With that? Like hell you are!" Olsen pushed him out of the way and Cade watched with not a little amusement as the other man bent over and examined the lock. Satisfied with whatever it was he saw, Olsen removed a small black leather case from a pocket of his fatigue pants and unzipped it, selecting two small metal tools from inside it. He stuck the ends of both into the lock, fished around with them for a couple of seconds, and then, with a satisfied grunt, removed them.

Grinning, he stuck a finger in the keyhole and pulled.

The door swung open soundlessly on well-oiled hinges.

Inside, they found the small gold container that was used to store the left-over Host after Mass. Cade took it out and handed it to Olsen; he knew instinctively that what he was looking for wasn't inside it. Martin considered his priestly duties to be sacred and he never would have compromised the Eucharist by storing anything in with the Host.

But the tabernacle itself was fair game.

The interior of the small container was lined with black velvet, making it impossible to see anything in the dim light of the church. Cade ran his gloved hands against the velvet, looking for something stashed away inside the small space, and was only mildly surprised when his fingers encountered the hidden switch.

"Heads up," he called to the others and then pushed it.

Glancing around, they all waited for something to happen.

Nothing did.

Cade frowned, pushed it again, and then did so a third time when everything still looked the same as it had before.

"Think it's broken?" Olsen asked.

"No. I just think we're not looking in the right spot." He turned to the others. "Spread out. It's here somewhere; I'm sure of it."

And it was. The switch activated a panel in the back of the wardrobe closet in the sacristy, revealing a staircase. Riley found it completely by chance; he was standing near the wardrobe when Cade flipped the switch for what must have been the twentieth time and heard the slight hiss the panel made as it slid open.

Cade had to give whoever built the place credit. It was a clever set-up. Securing the controls inside the tabernacle ensured that no one was going to trip the mechanism by accident and even if, by some strange circumstance, they did, nothing untoward would happen to give it away.

There was a switch just inside the doorway that activated a set of bulbs strung along the ceiling and by their light Echo Team's command squad descended. At the base of the steps they found a small chamber carved directly into the bedrock deep beneath the church.

A single bare bulb hung from a makeshift socket in the ceiling. Its harsh light illuminated the small space, giving them a good look at the altar of native stone that stood in the center of the room. A small chest rested on the altar, flanked by two fat, white church candles, the surface beneath them encrusted with the accumulation of years of melted wax. Next to the candle was a modern lighter.

As they spread out through the room, the light sent their shadows dancing across the walls and drew their attention to the mural painted on the one behind the altar. The mural stretched from floor to ceiling, covering a space about ten feet square, and showed an image of a rock-strewn plain of grey that stretched out to a horizon where storm clouds gathered. It was a landscape without a focus, as if the artist had completed only the background and had yet to begin the subject of the painting itself.

Cade knew better, however.

He knew it was a finished image, knew that the artist had actually captured the bleak nature of the place quite well. He'd been there, had plenty of first-hand experience to make the necessary comparison.

What he didn't know was what an image of the Beyond was doing on the wall of a room hidden beneath the church.

"Commander? I think you'd better have a look at this."

He turned to find Olsen had opened the chest and was staring at its contents, a strange combination of amazement and disgust plain on his face. Cade stepped up beside him.

Inside the chest, a mummified human hand rested on a bed of red silk.

Cade reached inside and carefully drew it out of the box, wanting to get a better look.

The hand had been severed about an inch below the wrist, providing a sort of handle with which to grasp it. A white, tallow like substance coated the fingers, covering the blackened skin beneath, and gave off the thick scent of animal fat and candle wax.

As the other men caught sight of the hand, Duncan crossed himself and a whispered prayer fell from Riley's lips.

Cade didn't blame them. The Hand of Glory was a potent piece of black magick, the kind of artifact that any self-respecting member of the church would avoid like the plague. Formed from the severed left hand of a murderer hung for his crime, the Hand could be used for all manner of nefarious purposes. The Order actually had two in their possession, the first taken from a warlock who'd used it to put an entire complement of Templar soldiers to sleep when they'd stormed his stronghold, the other removed from the grave of a sixteenth century mystic that had been unearthed during routine street repair in the White Chapel district of London three years before, both of them were secured under heavy guard to keep them from falling into the wrong hands.

Just what on earth had Father Martin been up to?

Cade began mentally cataloguing all of the uses of a Hand of Glory.

Putting your enemies to sleep.

Locating a missing person or object.

Forcing a confession from the servant of a witch.

Opening any lock. Or any door.

Wait a minute!

Cade looked from the Hand, to the mural, and back to the Hand again, suspicions flaring.

He grabbed the lighter from the altar top, clicked it on, and touched the flame to the tip of each finger, lighting each one like a candle. The stink of burning animal fat filled the room.

"Wait a minute…" Duncan began.

But Cade wasn't listening. He suspected he knew just what Father Martin was doing with the Hand of Glory, but the only way to be certain was to try it himself.

Praying he was wrong, Cade turned to the mural and pointed the Hand's burning fingers in the direction of the mural.

Something passed between the Hand and the wall, a force that was felt more than seen. The effects, however, became visible, as the entire painting shimmered like a mirage seen under the desert sun and then reformed once more, transforming the mural into a glistening web of arcane energy.

It was a portal.

And from the scene on the other side it was clear just where that portal would take them.

Into the heart of the Beyond.

CHAPTER 13

"SECRETS"

CADE STARED AT THE PORTAL with a mixture of amazement and disgust. Amazed that someone had apparently managed to create a permanent link to the Beyond when, by its very nature, the Beyond was always shifting and changing, never the same thing twice and disgusted that they had bothered to do so at all, for try as he might he couldn't think of a single worthwhile reason for doing so.

It appeared he was going to have to reevaluate not only what he knew about the Beyond, but about Father Martin as well.

Leaving the portal open was an invitation for any manner of creatures to come crawling across the Veil, so he waved the Hand of Glory at the wall a second time and then snuffed out the flames burning on the fingertips. As the last one was extinguished the wall shifted before their eyes once more, returning to its former, solid state.

It was looking more and more like they were going to have to chance making an incursion into the Beyond to determine just what Father Martin had been using the connection for. If they could open the portal from this side, there was also the chance that someone, or something, else could open it from the other, which meant they were going to have to post a guard for the time being, until they could decide just what to do about it.

Just what did you get yourself into, old man?

Leaving Riley and Olsen to keep an eye on the gate, Cade climbed back up the stairs, pulling out his cell phone as he went. Back in the sanctuary, he began making a series of phone calls.

His first one was to the duty officer at the Ravensgate Commandery, who he had transfer him to Echo's barracks. There he had someone track down Davis, First Squad's new leader. Cade had promoted him in the wake of Ortega's death inside the Eden complex and so far, Davis had been doing fairly well. Cade was confident that, given a bit more time, he'd fit into the role as if he'd been born to it. Once Davis picked up the phone, Cade let him know that he was ordering First and Second Squads to grab their kits and meet him at his current location in Boston as soon as possible, knowing that Davis would relay the information to Wilson, Second Squad's leader.

Regardless of what he found on the other side, Cade knew they were going to need back-up to handle the task of guarding the portal. You couldn't mount a round the clock operation with just four men. By getting the ball rolling now, he was increasing his options for later, and Cade liked to be prepared wherever and whenever he could. It was one of the traits that had made him so successful as Echo's leader.

That done, Cade hung up and took a moment to consider what he intended to say before dialing the Preceptor's direct line. It rang for a few times before Johansson's aide answered it.

"Preceptor's office. Nichols speaking."

"Knight Commander Williams for Preceptor Johannson."

"I'm sorry, Commander, the Preceptor is in a meeting at the moment and is currently unavailable."

Cade grinned. Just as he'd hoped. Now if the incompetent fool would only stay in meetings until this was over, things might actually go pretty smoothly.

"That's fine. Please let him know I called and that he can call me back whenever he finds a free moment."

"Very well, Knight Commander."

The aide's snobbish attitude was almost enough to match that of his boss. But Cade knew the message would be relayed almost verbatim, which was exactly what he wanted. The Preceptor didn't like him; that had been obvious from the start. He would consider any request from Cade that wasn't labeled as urgent to be of no consequence and would ignore it out of sheer spite.

Which would leave Cade to do as he pleased. Just as he'd hoped.

Closing his flip phone, Cade turned away, intending to return to the crypt hidden below the church, but then stopped, took his phone back out, and dialed another number. The phone rang and rang, heightening his anxiety, but at last it was answered. "What?"

Cade wasn't surprised by the greeting; it was how Clearwater always answered the phone. "It's me again," he said, knowing she would recognize his voice. If she didn't already know it was him calling. Sometimes her abilities made him seem damned normal.

She didn't sound thrilled to hear from him. "Did something happen? Did the wards collapse?"

"Oh, no. No, nothing like that. I just need your services

again."

She was silent for a time and then, "You didn't dig another one up, did you?"

"God no!" he said, trying to keep the humor out of his voice. Did she think he made a hobby of this? "I've been called away on urgent business and I can't make it back home again for several days. I need someone to watch over her until I get back."

There was silence on the other end of the line.

"I'll pay you double your normal rate to just sit there and keep an eye on her. I'll be back in a few days and that will be it. I won't drag you into this again."

She was against it, but after a bit more pleading she finally agreed. "Fine. A few days, no more."

She hung up without saying goodbye. Cade wasn't surprised. Clearwater might be the best hedge witch he knew, but she wasn't comfortable around people and her social skills were less than developed.

No matter. She knew her job and she would protect Gabrielle until he could get back there to do it himself.

With that taken care of, he turned and made his way back down the stairs to the room below. It was time to begin preparations for a short trip through the portal into the Beyond.

They had to find out what Father Martin had been involved with and passing through the portal was the quickest way to discover that information.

CHAPTER 14

"ON THE OTHER SIDE"

CADE NORMALLY WOULD HAVE MADE the trip across the Veil on his own, but this time he wasn't comfortable with that idea. Just about anything at all could be waiting for them on the other side and he wanted not only another set of eyes and ears to be certain he didn't miss anything, but also someone who could carry what they learned back to the Order should something happen to him.

As executive officer, Riley had to stay behind and manage the unit while Cade was gone. Duncan had been across the Veil before, but finding the portal beneath a church clearly had him shaken up and Cade didn't think dragging him through it was the best thing right now.

Which left Olsen.

With the decision made, Cade rejoined the others in the secret room below the church and filled them in on his intentions.

"We need a better understanding of why this portal exists and what Father Martin used it for before we report the discovery to high command. The only way to do that is to go through it and scout around a bit on the other side. Once we do, we'll have a better idea of how the Order needs to react.

"Olsen, you're with me. Suit up, but leave your firearms behind. They don't work on the other side anyway. Swords and knives only. We leave in ten minutes."

As Olsen headed up the stairs to retrieve their kit bags from where they'd left them in the church above, Cade turned to the other two. "You two are on guard duty. Give us a couple of hours. If we're not back by then, report in and let the Seneschal know about the portal."

With the orders given, there wasn't anything left to do but gear up and get things under way.

Olsen and Cade stood before the reactivated gate, with Riley and Duncan at their backs. The knight commander turned to face his companion.

"You'll feel some resistance as you pass through the gate, but just push through it and you'll be fine. I'll go first and will be waiting for you on the other side."

Without waiting for an answer, Cade faced the gate, drew his sword, and took the last several steps needed to carry him into the shimmering portal. There was a moment of bitter cold and a sense of absolute abandonment so profound that if he hadn't been expecting it, Cade would have curled up in a corner and wept.

He found himself standing inside the ruins of a small room. The hazy illumination that passed for sunlight was filtering in through a nearby doorway, giving Cade just enough light to see by. The ceiling above his head had partially collapsed and if he hadn't come through the portal hunched over slightly he probably would have smacked his head on it. He turned to face the portal and through its shifting shimmering surface he could just make out the hazy forms of Olsen and Riley standing on the other side. Lifting a hand, he gave the signal and then stepped away from the portal, making room for Olsen, who came through moments later.

Olsen was shaking violently when he emerged and Cade gave him a moment to gather his wits. The passage through the Veil was never an easy one and that space between worlds could feel like forever to the uninitiated. Cade had made the trip multiple times while searching for Gabrielle and had become hardened to the experience, but aside from their encounter with the angel Baraquel, who had thrown Echo's entire command unit violently across the gap, this was Olsen's only trip into the Beyond and Cade knew it would be disconcerting, to say the least.

"You okay?" Cade asked after a moment.

Olsen nodded. "That was a bit freakier than I expected, but I'll be okay in a minute." His voice shook slightly when he spoke, but his shivering had stopped and the panicked expression seemed to have left his face, at least for the time being.

"Good. I'd hate to have to embarrass you in front of the other men by sending you back."

"Fat chance of that," Olsen replied and this time he had himself under control.

Satisfied, Cade crossed the room to the doorway and looked out. Olsen joined him.

The Beyond was still very much a mystery to Cade, despite his many journeys there. As nearly as he could tell, it was a shadow realm that existed close to the real world in time and space, but forever separated by a wall of energy he had come to call the Veil. Like the mystical Purgatory, it was inhabited by the shades of the dead, those that for one reason or another had not moved on to a more lasting rest. Other creatures inhabited the Beyond as well, dark, twisted creatures of all shapes and sizes, and one had to be on their guard at all times while journeying there.

To make matters worse, the landscape of the Beyond was constantly shifting. Like a funhouse mirror, it had a tendency to make things appear either hauntingly familiar or intimately strange. This side of the Veil could often seem to be be a mirror image of the other, except here the passage of entropy marked everything with a patina of decay. Cade liked to think of it as a photograph and its negative image.

Sometimes, though, the Beyond was simply *different.*

Like now.

In the real world, the church under which the portal was situated was in the midst of a suburban neighborhood, surrounded by other buildings, from two-family homes to the local grocery.

But here, that wasn't the case.

Before them stretched a sea of what could only be called vegetation, though it was unlike any vegetation any human had ever seen. Dark and twisted, it hung across everything in its path like a spider's web, seeming to squeeze everything in its iron grip. Looking behind them, they could see that the shell of the building from which they had emerged was covered with it. In fact, it was the growth that had caused the collapse of the structure, the heavy bows forcing the roof partially down into the rest of the building.

A path led down the small hill on which the church rested to what appeared to be a roadway, both of which had been carved from the center of the vegetation. Cade could see burn marks along the edge of the path, evidence that it had been cleared recently, and there were faint tracks in the dirt beneath their feet.

With no other direction available to them, they set out along the path.

They hadn't gone far when a faint whispering reached their ears.

"Hear that?" Olsen asked, unnerved.

"It's just the wind," Cade replied absently, but then stopped.

The wind wasn't blowing.

He turned in a slow circle, looking for movement, hoping to catch sight of something moving toward them through the vegetation.

"Can you tell where it's coming from?"

Olsen shook his head. He was glancing around as well, one hand on the hilt of his sword.

Out of the corner of his eye, Cade saw motion and he spun in that direction. He was just in time to see a lengthy piece of vine slide out across the path ahead of them. As if sensing his scrutiny, it suddenly went limp. If he hadn't been looking right at it, Cade would have convinced himself that it had only been a trick of the light.

But he *had* been looking.

And it hadn't been the light.

"Cover me," he said softly.

Olsen stepped closer, sword drawn, while Cade drew an emergency flare from the cargo pocket of his utilities and, with a flick of one hand, activated it.

The flare blazed to life, its flame a strange mix of white and grey rather than the usual red. From previous travels Cade knew the flame would make him sick to his stomach if he stared at it too long so he avoided looking at it, turning his attention instead to the vegetation lining the path.

Once it was lit, he held the flare in one hand and drew his sword with the other. Striding forward, he thrust the flame at the vine that had flopped across their path.

Faster than a striking snake, the vine whipped itself back into the dense foliage behind it. One minute it was there, the next it was not.

Olsen gaped at Cade. "Are you freakin' kidding me?"

The Knight Commander shook his head. "Afraid not. I'd say that's a pretty good indication we should stick to the path, wouldn't you?"

Following his example, Olsen lit a flare of his own and the two of them continued on their journey, moving down the path. A little later they reached the wider road. It ran perpendicular to their current direction and from the tracks beneath their feet it was clear that the traffic had been moving to the left only.

They had come to find out who or what was using the portal, Cade followed the tracks.

Ruined buildings could now be seen beneath the vegetation on either side of the road and, putting two and two together, Cade understood just what had happened to the "neighborhood" around the church. This was a mirror image of the reality that existed on the other side of the Veil, except in this case, the vegetation had grown abnormally large and had developed a sentience of its own. It had swallowed the town whole, smothering it beneath a sea of creeping vines.

Everything but the road.

Someone was keeping it open.

But for what?

As they walked the whispering followed them, slowly growing in volume. When it grew too loud Cade would brandish the flare and the vines would settle down again, but they didn't stay silent for long. It took the two men twenty minutes and three flares a piece to reach the end of the growth. Both were happy to leave it behind. With only five more flares between them, they were going to have to be more conservative on the way back.

Ahead of them rose a series of rugged hills covered with a dense growth of forest. The road continued up and over them, passing through the trees. Both men were leery about entering the woods, but they discovered that the trees were just ordinary. Whatever had animated the vegetation in the valley behind them had apparently been restricted to that area, much to their relief.

As they climbed higher, they began to see the ruins of buildings here and there among the trees. Curiosity eventually got the better of them and they began making occasional detours to check out particularly interesting locales. More often than not there wasn't much left, just a series of walls open to the sky above, and the occasional piece of furniture that had survived the ravages of the elements and whatever denizens of the Beyond that made the forest their home.

During one such stop, Olsen froze suddenly and raised his hand for silence.

"Listen!" Olsen whispered.

Cade did so and from the ridgeline came the muted sounds of activity, though they were too far away to assess what it might be.

They left the ruins behind and climbed up the lee side of the ridge as quietly as possible. As they drew close to the rim, they got down on their bellies and crawled. At the top they carefully peered over the edge.

Below them, spread out across the valley floor, was a large encampment spread out amongst more ruins like those they had just left behind. Cade counted thirty tents, each one with round sides and a sloping roof, similar to a Mongolian yurt. They appeared easy to set up and take down and probably didn't require too much effort to transport. A large structure could also be seen in the center of the camp, consisting of several tents strung together, their rectangular styles in sharp contrast to the circular ones around them. Figures moved about the camp, but they were too far away to be seen clearly.

Olsen was prepared. He pulled a pair of mini-binoculars from the cargo pouch on his pants and took a long look through them. Without a word, he passed them to Cade.

From the expression on Olsen's face, Cade knew it couldn't be good.

He took a look for himself.

The camp was full of Chiang Shih.

They were making preparations for something. From the size and number of the boxes and crates that were being moved about the camp, it was clearly a major undertaking.

Cade knew that the Chiang Shih were typically solitary creatures and it took either a strong militant commander or the promise of lush hunting grounds to bring even a handful of them together as a group. To assemble a force of this size, the prize must be particularly attractive.

Like the entire city of Boston.

"There has to be a hundred and fifty, maybe two hundred of them down there," Olsen whispered.

But Cade barely heard him. His attention had been caught by a familiar face and he shifted position, doing what he could to keep the individual in sight while focusing the binoculars for a better look.

Olsen noticed Cade's change in intensity.

"What is it?"

Cade didn't answer, not yet, wanting to be sure before he said anything, but then he finally had the glasses focused the way he wanted and there was no question about the individual's identity.

Bishop.

He handed the glasses back to his companion.

"About ten yards in front of that main structure and a couple feet to the left."

"What? I don't see...son-of-a-bitch!" He looked at Cade. "There he is."

Cade nodded. What he would have done for an operational sniper rifle at that point.

He caught Olsen's eye and with a nod of his head indicated that they should get going. Olsen silently agreed and the two men made their way back off the ridge and moved away from the Chiang Shih encampment.

When they were out of earshot, they spent a few minutes discussing the situation. It seemed obvious that the road continued around the ridge and passed through the center of the town that the Chiang Shih had claimed as their own. If they used the ruins they'd just left behind as a staging area and had enough reinforcements, they might be able to get into position for a strike at the camp without being seen, though a lot would depend on good timing and a healthy dose of luck.

Either way, it was clear that they had to get back to the other side of the Veil and inform the Order of what they had seen. The decision as to what to do about the Chiang Shih would be made by others higher in the Order's hierarchy and for that both men were grateful, but they didn't fool themselves into thinking they wouldn't be part of the solution.

There was a fight coming and Echo was bound to be at the

vanguard of it.

It was time to get back and warn the others of what they had seen. With a last glance toward the ridgeline and the threat that lay just beyond, Cade turned and headed back down through the woods toward the road with Olsen at his heels.

* * *

After the men had left, a shadow detached itself from a nearby tree and stood upright. It had been hard pressed not to feed on the life force that had been so tantalizingly close, but the warlord had been clear on what would happen to any that did so.

Knowing they were here was enough. The warlord would offer a generous reward when he heard the news.

Thrilled by its good fortune, the shadow moved to the nearest patch of darkness and disappeared within.

CHAPTER 15

"A DECISION MADE"

I MMEDIATELY UPON THEIR RETURN CADE sent out a request for a meeting with the North American Preceptor, Willem Johansson, and the Seneschal of the Order, Jacob MacIntyre.

Second only to the Grand Master, the Seneschal ran the Order's day-to-day operations and was the true power behind the throne. Cade, and by extension Echo itself, worked directly for the Seneschal, circumventing the usual hierarchy where the local special ops team reported to their home Preceptor. While he didn't need to include Johansson, the operation Cade was about to request was on his turf and Cade was trying to play nice by including the Preceptor in his notification of pending action. The Seneschal would listen to Johansson input, but Cade knew MacIntrye would ultimately choose to follow Cade's advice, and so having the other man involved couldn't hurt anything.

It took about an hour to make the necessary arrangements in

Scotland and to set up the equipment Cade needed in his hotel room in Boston. He sent the rest of his team out to get a bite to eat, powered up his laptop, made sure the camera was working properly, and then dialed out.

On the other side of the Atlantic, in a secure room in the ancestral castle Rosslyn, a young acolyte accepted the connection. A moment later Cade's screen split into two separate video streams. The first was his own, showing how he appeared to the people on the other end. The second was the answering stream from the Seneschal's office and Jacob's ruddy face soon filled half of the screen.

"Do you have any idea what time it is over here, Knight Commander?" MacIntyre asked gruffly, though not without kindness.

The question stumped Cade for a moment, for he hadn't even considered the issue before this. He did some quick calculations in his head. If it were just after seven p.m., and Scotland was roughly seven hours ahead of the east coast of the US, then it would be...about two a.m. there.

"My apologies Seneschal, but I felt this couldn't wait."

"Well, at least you've got the grace to appear embarrassed," MacIntyre said humorously, when Cade appeared anything but. "What is so important that you had to drag an old man from his sleep?"

Cade paused. "Is Preceptor Johansson with us?" he asked. He didn't want to repeat the information.

His screen split again and the Preceptor's face appeared in the new window. "I'm right here, Knight Commander. I, too, trust that this is important?"

Pompous prick, Cade thought, but kept his face calm and non-threatening. One day that man will get his..."I assure you

99

both that it is." Cade went on to detail the events of the past few days, bringing them two men up to speed with regard to the request for help from Father Martin, their arrival in Boston only to find that Father Martin had been murdered, and their subsequent discovery of the room and its secret portal deep beneath the church.

He left out just how they'd found the secret entrance to the room or what they'd done to activate the portal. While the Seneschal knew about his particular talents, Cade didn't like giving fuel to the perception that he was a heretic.

"I am assuming you investigated the area on the other side of this portal?" asked the Seneschal.

"Yes, sir," Cade replied and couldn't help but grin inwardly at the surprised expression on Preceptor Johansson's face at his revelation of prior action.

"And?" prompted the Seneschal.

"We discovered a large force of Chiang Shih assembled nearby and a good degree of traffic from their base to the portal itself. Evidence suggests that they are planning to launch an assault on the Greater Boston area, similar to the attempt that was made back in 2003."

"What 'evidence' are you talking about?" asked the Preceptor. Cade couldn't tell if the man's annoyance was directed at him or at the Shadows for daring to think they could come into territory he considered his personal fiefdom.

Cade let a hint of condescension creep into his tone, in case it was the former. "The Shadows are not, by nature, cooperative creatures. It takes an extremely powerful war leader to make them band together for even the best of reasons. Expanding their territory would be at the top of that list."

"Why couldn't they simply be expanding into the Beyond?"

Cade laughed; he couldn't help it. "If you'd ever seen the Beyond, Preceptor, you wouldn't need to ask that question. There isn't a more barren place I can think of and there certainly isn't anything to sustain them there." He turned to face the Seneschal again. "No, the only reason they are there at all is to make use of that portal to strike where we least expect it."

"What do you suggest we do?"

"Assemble a force big enough to take them on and do it quickly," Cade replied without hesitation.

The Seneschal gave that some thought. "I agree with you that a Chiang Shih gathering of that size is a definite threat, but I don't understand why we have to face them in open combat. Why not simply shut down the portal?"

Cade had been expecting that line of questioning and he didn't hesitate to address it. "With all due respect, sir, leaving a force of that size combat ready is not a good idea. We don't have any understanding of how the gate came to be or what will be necessary to close it permanently. Destroying the building might do the trick, but then again it might not. And what's to keep them from simply relocating and trying again? We wouldn't have any idea where they were. How would we stop them then? Our best move is to eliminate the effectiveness of the fighting force entirely, assuring we won't have to worry about them again in the future."

And ending the problem of Bishop once and for all, he added silently. Cade had purposely not mentioned him. He considered Bishop's involvement to be a personal matter, something he'd left unresolved and which he intended to handle at the first opportunity.

The Preceptor had a sour expression on his face, but Cade ignored it. The Seneschal controlled the Order's fighting units and he was the one Cade had to convince.

MacIntyre conferred with someone off-screen for a few moments and then addressed Cade.

"Unfortunately, our teams are scattered to hell and back right now. Assembling a force powerful enough to take on the Chiang Shih will require some time. Delta is still dealing with that mess in Greenland and Charlie is on furlough. Alpha and Baker can't be taken off their current assignments. Which means we need Echo to keep the enemy off balance long enough to buy us the time we need to bring men in from the field. Can you do that?"

Cade nodded. "With your permission, I'll take a small raiding party back across the Veil and begin harassing their camp. Standard guerilla warfare hit-and-run tactics. The resulting confusion should be enough to disrupt their timetable and give us the time we need to assemble our own forces to face them head on."

"And the portal?"

"I'll leave a squad or two in reserve at the church. The portal is small and the room is also. The enemy will only be able to bring a few soldiers across at a time. We should be able to hold them off until help arrives."

The Seneschal inclined his head in that way that Cade knew meant he was thinking things over. Cade waited patiently, trying not to look too anxious. His gut told him that acting quickly and decisively was the best way of dealing with this. If they waited too long, things would certainly get out of hand.

When the Seneschal finally gave him permission to carry out his plan, Cade made sure to keep the smile of satisfaction from his face.

CHAPTER 16

"BRIEFING"

C ADE WAS WAITING OUTSIDE WHEN First and Second
Squad arrived. He had them park the SUVs behind
the church in the rear parking lot and helped them
carry the equipment in through the storage room. Riley and
Olsen were already suited up, so they took lights downstairs
while the rest of the men assembled in the sanctuary and quickly
donned the equipment needed for the mission ahead of them.

A set of dark ceramic body armor, blessed by the Holy
Father, went on first, followed by a black jumpsuit of flame-
retardant material. Normally each man would carry an HK Mark
23 .45 caliber handgun in a shoulder holster, but these were
discarded today in favor of their combat knives and swords. The
former were worn in either wrist or ankles sheaths and the
swords were worn in specially designed scabbards across each
team member's backs, the hilts readily accessible over one
shoulder or the other. Lightweight Kevlar tactical helmets with

built-in communications gear, including video and audio recording devices, went on last.

When they were ready, Cade passed through the ranks, inspecting each man, joking with them, offering a word of encouragement here and there when he felt it was needed. When he was finished they filed into the pews for the benediction and communion offering.

It was Cade's intention to take one additional squad besides the men in the command unit. That was it. Eight men total. No vehicles, no extra troops, nothing to limit their speed or reaction time. Their intent was to harass the enemy and for that speed was crucial. Cade had no intention of getting into a long, drawn-out battle if it could be avoided. In fact, he would do everything in his power to be sure it didn't happen.

First and Second Squads drew straws to see who would go and who would stay. Second lost and so Cade ordered them into a defensive position around the portal with orders to shoot anything that came through that wasn't a part of the Order.

After Second Squad had filed out of the room, Cade addressed the rest of the men remaining in the group. He told them what they had found downstairs, what he intended to do about the discovery, and what to expect in the process.

"We're about to leave this plane of existence behind and step into another one. The barrier between the two realms is called the Veil. Physically, you'll feel a brief sense of dislocation and weightlessness when you cross it. It's entirely normal and I'm telling you about it now so you don't freak out when it happens in the midst of transit. Just stay calm and relax. It will go away in a few seconds.

"Emotionally it's another matter. Everyone reacts differently to the crossing and I can't predict what it will feel like for you.

But no matter how you feel, remember that it's only temporary. Stay focused on your faith and on the mission and you'll be fine.

"Where we are going doesn't have a formal name. Over the years, I've simply come to call it the Beyond. It's like a mirror world of this one, except over there, emotion is the big differentiator, not technology. Your firearms won't work, so don't even bother bringing them along; they'll just be dead weight. Keep your swords handy and if you've got an extra combat knife it wouldn't hurt to have it close.

"The more force, willpower, and sheer determination you put into a strike, the better the outcome. If you don't believe in what you are doing, the most perfectly executed slash to the enemy's throat will only serve to draw a little blood rather than take the man's head off. So stay focused and put everything you have into each and every swing."

Cade paused and looked them over, confident that they were the right men for the job.

They all met his gaze squarely and without hesitation.

"You're going to experience a change in your vision over there. All the color will be leached away. Everything, and I do mean everything, will be seen in some shade of grey. Once you come back to this side of the Veil, things will return to normal, so don't panic when it happens. The one exception to this might be each one of us – in the Beyond, the living often seem to come across as more colorful, more vibrant than the dead."

Cade caught Simpson, a man who'd joined Echo after Callevechio's demise a few months earlier, looking a bit green around the gills and nodded encouragingly. "Those of you who were with me on the Eden op spent several days in the Beyond and escaped unscathed, so you know what to expect. Help the new men through the portal and stay with them until they've gotten used to things on the other side.

"Our mission is to disrupt the Chiang Shih encampment, buying time for the Order to mobilize enough troops to deal with what we expect to be a major incursion. We strike hard, strike fast, and then fade into the mountains, waiting for the next chance to do it all over again.

"Some of you have fought the Chiang Shih before. You know how fast and utterly ruthless they are. For the rest of you, understand that the enemy is driven by one thing only – hunger. They feed off the life force of the living and they need to do so again and again in order to sustain themselves. You're going to look like a five course meal to them, since the living are few and far between in the Beyond. Stick together. Don't let them drag you off alone."

He paused, gave them a moment to digest what he'd said, and then asked, "Questions?"

There weren't any, so Cade let Riley take over. Echo's exec got the men on their feet, double-checked their gear, and then marched them out of the room and down the stairs to stand single file in front of the portal.

Casting one last look at the crucifix hanging above the altar and saying a short prayer, Cade turned and walked off after them, his thoughts no longer on the here and now but on what they would find once they crossed the Veil into the Beyond.

With Second Squad's men in position, and the men from First Squad and the Command Unit packed into the room, there was very little space left to move around. Cade squeezed his way past the altar and stepped up next to the portal, to where Riley stood waiting for him. The portal itself had already been opened.

"Ready?" Cade asked.

"Always," Riley replied and Cade knew he meant it. The

Master Sergeant was one of the best men he'd ever served with and he always felt better facing the unknown knowing the big man had his back.

"All right, I'll go through first. You should be able to see me once I emerge on the other side. At my signal start sending them through one at a time after that, a minute or so between each one. You bring up the rear."

"Roger that, boss."

"Good. I'll see you on the other side."

Drawing his sword, Cade walked over to the portal and without hesitation stepped through its shimmering surface.

CHAPTER 17

"WELCOME TO THE OTHER SIDE"

ONE BY ONE, THEY CAME through after him. Some of them crossed the Veil without incident. A few reacted just as Olsen had, overcome by their emotions, and needed a few minutes to find their equilibrium. Childers, one of the new men from First Squad, was violently sick when he came through, vomiting repeatedly for the better part of five minutes, but some salt tablets and a few gulps of water from his canteen seemed to settle him down and Cade let him stay with the unit.

All in all, it was better than Cade anticipated. He gave them a few minutes to get used to the reality around them, knowing from personal experience how disconcerting it could be and then got them organized into position to move out.

Nightfall was a few hours away and he wanted to have them in a secure position before then. All sorts of creatures roamed the Beyond after dark and the men from Echo didn't need to waste their time or energy fighting any foe other than the Chiang Shih. By setting up a defensive position in the ruins that he and Olsen had located on their previous journey, they should be able to stay low and avoid any of the roaming denizens of the dark while at the same time planning their campaign against the Chiang Shih in the valley below.

They headed out, moving in single file down the path until they reached the wider street below. They stopped for a moment to light the gasoline torches that they'd brought along with them. Cade wasn't thrilled with the fact that the flames would also serve as a beacon, revealing their presence to anyone who might be watching, but he'd been unable to come up with any other way, short of using a flamethrower, to get such a large group through the gauntlet posed by the vegetation around them. The torches would burn longer than the flares they used previously and wouldn't be as noticeable as the curtain of fire a flamethrower would create. And they should serve nicely to keep the creeping vines away from their route until they reached the far side of town.

As they walked Cade noted that something about the landscape around them was different.

There was color here.

Not just in his men, which was to be expected, for the living were always brighter than anything else on the other side of the Veil, but in all that he looked at, from the subtle hues of brown working their way through the dirt beneath his feet to the streaks of green and black that ran through the carpet of vegetation spread out before them.

It was as if the living world was somehow leaking into the Beyond.

What the hell was going on?

The last few days had been filled with their share of surprises. First his conversation with Logan, quickly followed by his discovery that Gabrielle was still lingering on in some sort of suspended state of existence and that everything Logan had told him about the Adversary and his plans for Gabrielle might actually be true. Then he'd received the mysterious package from Father Martin, which had led them to the church, the portal, and the current mission into the Beyond.

Something deep in his gut told him that the two groups of events were somehow linked together, that what had happened to Gabrielle was in some way connected to the events involving Father Martin, but he couldn't make sense of it all yet, couldn't find the forest for the trees around him, it seemed. He needed some time to sit back and think about it, work it through in his head, but time was luxury he just didn't have.

They left the remains of the town behind without incident and continued their march. It took them another hour to climb through the hilly country just beyond, finally reaching the particular ridgeline they'd selected as their staging area just before nightfall.

Cade had the men scout the surrounding area, making certain that they were alone. Once they had returned and given the all-clear, he had them set up three guard posts in a triangle formation around the camp, each one about fifty yards away from the center. That would give them enough warning if something managed to breach the perimeter.

An uncomfortable incident occurred just after they'd settled into camp, when the men broke out their rations. Like most modern military units, the Templars used MREs, or Meals Ready to Eat, individual packaged meals with a self-contained heating device inside. Each man had several MREs with them in their packs. But every package that they opened turned out to be spoiled, filled with maggots and other unidentifiable insects. They also stank to high heaven, as if the food inside had been spoiled for days, which should have been impossible since all of the packages were of recent manufacture and were sealed tightly up until the moment the troops opened them. Only the crackers and drink mix were still edible.

It was a disturbing reminder of where they were and several of them men crossed themselves and said a short prayer as the information was passed around. More than one refused to touch the crackers or the drink mix, and Cade knew that this was going to be a much larger problem come the morning when they needed food to keep their energy levels up after an attack on the Chiang Shih encampment.

Still wondering what to do about it, Cade moved off to a quiet corner and tried to get some sleep.

* * *

He stands alone in the center of the street, in a town that has no name. He has been here before, more than once, but each time the resolution is different, as if the events about to transpire are ordained by the random chance found on a giant spinning wheel, a cosmic wheel of fortune, and not by the actions he is about to take or has taken before.

He knows from previous experience that, just a few blocks beyond this one the town suddenly ends, becoming a great plain of nothingness, the landscape an artist's canvas that stands untouched, unwanted.

This town has become the center of his universe.

Around him, the blackened buildings sag in crumbling heaps, testimony to his previous visits. He wonders what the town will look like a few weeks from now, when the confrontation about to take place has been enacted and re-enacted and reenacted again, until even these ragged shells stand no more. Will the road, like the buildings, be twisted and torn?

He does not know.

He turns his attention back to the present, for even after all this time, he might learn something new that could lead him to his opponent's true identity.

The sky is growing dark, though night is still hours away. Dark grey storm clouds laced with green-and-silver lightning are rolling in from the horizon, like horses running hard to reach the town's limits before the fated confrontation begins. The air is heavy with impending rain and the electrical tension of the coming storm. In the slowly fading afternoon light the shadows around him stretch and move. He learned early on that they can have a life of their own.

He avoids them now.

The sound of booted feet striking the pavement catches his attention, and he knows he has exhausted his time here. He turns to face the length of the street before him, just in time to see his foe emerge from the crumbled ruins at its end, just as he has emerged each and every time they have encountered one another in this place. It is as if his enemy is always here, silently waiting with infinite patience for him to make his appearance.

Pain shoots across his face and through his hands, phantoms of the true sensation that had once coursed through his flesh, from their first meeting in another time and place. Knowing it will not last, he waits the few seconds for the pain to fade. Idly, he wonders, not for the first time, if the pain is caused by his foe or by his own recollection of the suffering he once endured at the enemy's hands.

He smiles grimly as the pain fades.

A chill wind suddenly rises, stirring the hairs on the back of his neck, and in that wind, he is certain he can hear the soft, sibilant whispers of a thousand lost souls, each and every one crying out to him to provide solace and sanctuary.

The voices act as a physical force, pushing him forward from behind, and before he knows it he is striding urgently down the street. His hands clench into fists as he is enveloped with the desire to tear his foe limb from limb with his bare hands. So great is his anger that it makes him forget the other weapons at his disposal in this strange half-state of reality.

The Adversary simply stands in the middle of the street, waiting. His features are hidden in the darkness of the hooded cloak that he wears over his form in this place, but his mocking laughter echoes clearly off the deserted buildings and carries easily in the silence.

The insult only adds fuel to Cade's rage.

Just as he draws closer, the scene shifts, wavers, the way a mirage will shimmy in the heat rising from the pavement. For a second it regains its form and in that moment Cade has the opportunity to glimpse the surprise in the other's face, then everything dissolves around him in a dizzying spiral of shifting patterns and unidentified shapes.

Cade came awake with a gasp, the now familiar dream putting his heart rate into overdrive.

But this time, he'd noticed something different.

Amidst the ruins surrounding the Adversary, Cade had seen vegetation that looked surprisingly like that which had covered the town they had passed through earlier that afternoon.

CHAPTER 18

"DEATH COMES A CALLIN'"

AFTER THE SEEMING REALITY OF the dream, Cade was unable to go back to sleep. He decided to make himself useful, so he got up and checked in by radio with the listening posts, knowing that they'd be happy to hear a friendly voice after being alone out there in the dark for awhile.

Posts one and two were doing just fine. He was in the midst of speaking with Davis, who was holed up in post three, when the other man interrupted in mid-sentence. "Hold on a sec, Commander. I think I see..."

Cade glanced out across the darkness in Davis' direction but he was too far away to see anything for himself. A minute passed, then two. He was about to call Davis back when the other man saved him the trouble.

"We've got incoming!" Davis shouted into the radio. "Twenty five to thirty Chiang Shih, maybe more. I lost count. I'm forty yards out and closing."

The men manning the listening posts had orders to hotfoot it back to camp if they came under attack and Davis was obviously following them. Cade was confident that he would make it in time. His warning would also give the team the time they needed to be ready before the enemy reached them.

"Stations!" Cade cried, rousing the rest of his troops and then scrambled to get into position himself.

As he did so, Cade found himself wondering how the Chiang Shih had known they were there. Had they missed a sentry? Tripped some kind of warning system? Was it just dumb bad luck?

They were about to face a force much larger than he'd ever intended they face and at a time and place not of their choosing. It was going to take all of their skill to get through this. But like any good commander, Cade had made sure his men knew what to do in the event of an attack on their encampment and they reacted as they'd been trained. Seconds after the warning from Davis, the team was lined up in a semi-circle facing the onrushing enemy, protected by the ruins at their back.

The bows worked as well as Cade had hoped, the act of physically drawing the bowstring infusing the weapon with enough personal emotion to allow them to operate within the confines of the Beyond. Shot after shot flew from the Templar ranks, each one unerringly finding its target as the enemy rushed out of the treeline before them.

But it wasn't enough.

The woods were full of Chiang Shih, with more and more appearing at every moment and it was clear to Cade that if they stayed where they were they would be overrun.

As much has he hated to give up this position, it hadn't been designed to withstand a full on attack. Trying to make a stand against this many of the enemy wasn't even an option. They were a guerilla force, not an army. They had no choice but to retreat back the way they had come. If they could reach the portal before they were cut off, they could rely on Second Squad and the rest of the men they'd left behind to cover their retreat and keep the enemy from crossing the Veil.

"Fall back!" Cade cried and like a well-oiled machine the Templars surged into motion, leapfrogging backward, one group covering the other as they made their way back through the trees toward the road below.

And just like that, his plan to harass and annoy the enemy went out the window.

The moon gave them enough light to see by and the team quickly reassembled on the road below. A few of the men had minor wounds, but nothing serious. Cade could only hope it stayed that way. A count was quickly taken and when they were certain they had everyone with them, they continued onward. Cade estimated they had maybe five minutes lead on the enemy. It wouldn't take the Chiang Shih long to figure out where they had gone and when they did, it would be a race to see who could reach the portal first.

Cade intended to win that race.

Free of the trees and the surrounding vegetation they made good time, reaching the outskirts of the town before too long.

That's where things took a turn for the worse.

A glow lit the horizon ahead of them. Cade had just noticed it when Riley came back down the line, an urgent look on his face.

"They've fired the town. If we don't move quickly, we'll be cut off."

His words were all it took to spur the men to redouble their efforts. They charged ahead, the thump of their booted feet the only sounds that passed between them. It wasn't long before the air was filled with the smell of smoke and burning vegetation , getting thicker as they continued forward.

As they neared the end of town flames could be seen rising high into the night sky. Cade felt like a rat in a maze and he wondered what they would find when they reached the other side; would the Chiang Shih be waiting for them? Why else would they fire the town, if not to drive them in a certain direction?

But neither he nor the Chiang Shih had remembered that the vegetation had a life of its own. And at that moment, it decided it had had enough.

All about them, the plants reared up, dragging themselves free of their roots and fleeing in whatever direction they could. The team was forced to slow down, hunting for paths through the flames that were likely to change with every passing moment.

Like any wounded animal the vegetation reacted blindly to the intense pain caused by the fire, rearing up around them and slamming itself back down, trying to put out the flames by beating itself against the ground.

Unfortunately, this only served to fan the fire.

A blazing wall of vegetation suddenly swept toward them and Cade was forced to dive to one side to avoid the flames. As he climbed to his feet he discovered that one of their number hadn't been so fortunate. While most of the team had thrown themselves to the left, Duncan had dived in the other direction and was now cut off by the surging flames.

To make matters worse the front ranks of the enemy had finally caught up to them. Realizing he couldn't reach Cade and the others, Duncan turned to face the enemy.

Alone.

Olsen didn't hesitate. Screaming Duncan's name, he charged through the growing fire, intent on saving his teammate.

The flames flared up again, preventing Cade from following, and he could only stand and watch and pray.

For a moment he lost sight of Olsen as he was obscured by the smoke and flames but then he reappeared, this time on the other side of the conflagration. One arm of his uniform was ablaze, but he ignored it, fighting like a demon from hell itself. His sword rose and fell, rose and fell, as he chopped and slashed his way through the ranks of the enemy.

Duncan must have taken heart at his appearance for his own struggles suddenly intensified as well. Like a man possessed he slashed at the Chiang Shih within reach, all the while deflecting the various blows that reigned down upon him.

For a moment Cade thought he might be witnessing a miracle, thought that the two men might prevail against the superior numbers and strength of the enemy surrounding them.

Please Lord, he thought.

But then it happened.

Olsen stumbled, his sword dipping slightly as he fought to maintain his balance, and one of the waiting Chiang Shih took advantage of the opening, reaching past the Templar's blade and slashing its razor sharp claws across Olsen's unprotected throat.

Blood and flesh flew.

Olsen jerked upright like a puppet on strings, his free hand going to the ruin of his throat. Cade could see the shock and surprise in the other man's gaze, could see the sudden awareness blossoming there that this was it, he'd fought his last battle, and there wouldn't be any last minute rescue.

Duncan must have seen it too, for he screamed in rage and pain and attempted to reach his wounded teammate.

It was no use.

With a final glance in Cade's direction, and perhaps a look of apology to go with it, Olsen collapsed and quickly disappeared beneath the swarming horde of the enemy.

With his death the fight seemed to go out of Duncan. He fought on for another moment, maybe two, before taking a savage blow to the back of his head and collapsing.

In the space of a heartbeat, Cade had lost two of his best men. *It's worse than that*, he thought. *He'd lost two of his friends.*

He couldn't believe it. It wasn't supposed to happen this way. They were supposed to have surprised the enemy, not the other way around. Olsen wasn't supposed to die. Neither was Duncan. They were supposed to be right here, fighting at his side, not lying bloody and cold amidst the ranks of the enemy....

Someone was shouting at him, pulling on his arm, and it took him a moment to refocus, to sweep the horrible image of his friends' death from his sight.

"We've got to get out of here! Now!" Riley shouted again.

The fire was almost upon them and if they stayed where they were another moment they'd perish as well, swallowed alive by the raging flames. Still Cade resisted. He stared through the smoke and flames, determined to know whether Duncan was alive or dead.

His diligence was rewarded. Through a break in the smoke he saw two of the enemy lift Duncan by his arms and begin dragging him off the field of battle. Duncan was struggling feebly against this captors, but the fight had clearly been beaten out of him. Cade didn't know why the Chiang Shih would want to keep the other man alive, but for now he was simply grateful that they did.

"Cade!" Riley yelled and this time Cade nodded to show he'd

understood and followed Riley as he led him down the narrow trail the others had taken, away from the inferno.

Hang on, Duncan, he thought, *just hang on. We'll be back for you.*

I promise.

CHAPTER 19

"QUESTIONS"

DUNCAN CLUNG TO CONSCIOUSNESS THE way a drowning man will cling to a life preserver, knowing that if he passed out he might never wake up again. His captors had him by the arms and were dragging him along so that his legs scraped against the rocky ground, the sharp stones tearing his clothing and digging into his flesh, but he was too weak to do anything but occasionally lift his head and look around.

They brought him down out of the hills and through the center of the Chiang Shih encampment. Faces loomed on all sides as they moved through the crowd. He was unable to focus on any of them, his pain and exhaustion pushing him to the limit. More than once he was struck from behind as he passed, but the blows were nothing compared to what he had already endured and so he ignored them, needing all of his energy to keep from passing out.

He was clearly losing the battle, for with a sort of dazed recognition he realized they had left the mob behind and were now inside a room. The walls were of concrete and in certain places he could see the steel rods that ran through them were the masonry had started to crumble and flake, but the room appeared structurally sound and the roof was intact. Duncan was dumped unceremoniously in the center of the floor. He landed on his wounded shoulder and the pain tore through him like a freight train, but it also served to clear his head and for that he was grateful.

He slowly pushed himself up by his hands and shook his head, clearing some of the cobwebs. He realized that the sound of the crowd outside was incredibly muted in here and he had a moment to wonder just how deep inside the building he actually was before a door on the other side of the room opened and someone joined them.

The man was tall and fit, which in a camp of warriors was to be expected, but unlike all of the other Chiang Shih that Duncan had seen so far this man was not of Asian descent. He was Caucasian, with blonde hair and blue eyes to match. An angry red scar ran across his throat, evidence of a close call at some point in the past.

He was dressed like a biker, in a dark shirt, leather pants and thick soled riding boots. But it was the ring on his right hand that drew Duncan's attention, the ring with a ruby stone in the shape of the Templar cross.

Seeing it, Duncan suddenly understood just who was behind this whole operation.

Bishop.

Cade's former teammate.

But what did he want with Echo?

Duncan suspected he was about to find out.

Bishop waved his hand and the two soldiers who had brought the prisoner in began to kick and beat him mercilessly. Given his current condition, it didn't take long for Duncan to pass out.

When he came to, however many minutes or hours later, he had no way of knowing, they started again. Their fists and boots slammed into him, striking his back, his stomach, his legs, his wounded shoulder, over and over again, until he couldn't take anymore and passed out again.

The third time around, he awoke to find himself alone in the room with Bishop. The other man sat on a stool close by, watching, and when he saw Duncan was awake he said, "Welcome back. I think it's time that you and I had a bit of a talk."

With a start, Duncan realized that he was secured against the wall, his arms and legs stretched out to either side and bound in manacles. The chains had been pulled so tight that he couldn't move.

He was utterly at the other man's mercy.

"I want to know the make-up and armament of all Templar units within the city limits. If you tell me what I want to know, I'll make things easier for you."

Duncan's mouth was so swollen and dry that he couldn't speak. Bishop called out in a language Duncan didn't understand and a few moments later another Chiang Shih entered the room carrying a bucket of water. Using a ladle he spooned out a few mouthfuls and dripped the water into Duncan's mouth.

Duncan swallowed, choked, and swallowed again. The water felt like heaven.

When he recovered his voice, he looked at Bishop and said carefully, "Fuck you."

The other man grinned.

"I was hoping you would say that."

He got up off the stool and walked slowly in Duncan's direction. As he did so, he held up one hand and Duncan could only watch in horror as the flesh on his limb began to shift and churn, transforming itself before his very eyes into a strange, jagged-edged instrument.

Bishop stood beside him, still grinning, and began to apply the edge of his newly formed limb to Duncan's tender flesh in a variety of ways.

Duncan's shrieks of pain went on for a long time.

CHAPTER 20

"DENIED"

THEY STAGGERED BACK THROUGH THE portal, carrying their wounded with them. Several of the Chiang Shih tried to follow, but Cade had left Second Squad deployed around the entrance for just that reason and the creatures were cut to pieces as soon as they came through the Veil. After a few attempts, they stopped coming.

Echo hadn't expected casualties, much less the deaths of several of their number, and Second Squad's medic was quickly overwhelmed. A call went out to the commandery for additional doctors, but it would take some time for anyone to get there and they would have to make do for the time being. In order to be certain his men were treated as expeditiously as possible, Cade ignored his own injuries and made certain the others were triaged correctly.

Cade was the last man treated when, an hour later, Preceptor Johannson walked into the back room they'd converted into make-shift hospital. The Knight Commander was in the process of relaying orders to Riley as the doctor bandaged his ribs and didn't notice the other man's entrance.

"...for now. Get a hold of Sullivan at Delta and see how many men he can spare. Then check with the armory at Ravensgate. I want to know how many more bows we can get our hands on in the time we have."

"Belay that order, Master Sergeant."

Cade looked over at him, surprised to see Johannson there.

"I'm sorry, Preceptor, I hadn't seen you come in. What did you say?"

"I told the Master Sergeant to strike your last order, as you won't need those weapons."

"If you have a better idea, please speak up. Firearms won't work on the other side of the Veil."

The Preceptor gave him a sour look. "I know very well what works and doesn't work, Knight Commander, but that's beside the point. You won't need the weapons because you won't be going back across the Veil."

The Preceptor's comment made so little sense that at first Cade suspected that he must have heard incorrectly. But on seeing the look on Riley's face, he knew that he hadn't. He felt his anger flare and couldn't hold back his tongue.

"What are you talking about? They've got Duncan! Of course we're going back!"

This time the Preceptor actually sneered. "You'll do as you're told, Knight Commander, and right now I'm telling you to stay away from that portal. There will be no further incursions into that hellish place except by my direct order."

Cade came out of his seat so quickly that the doctor stumbled backward.

"I'll go where I like and do what I like, Johannson. Or did you forget that that I don't take orders from you?"

"I'm well aware of the hierarchy that governs us, Williams. Which is why I asked the Seneschal to put your orders in writing." He reached inside his suit, took out a cream-colored envelope, and handed it to Cade.

The Knight Commander took the envelope and tore it open, extracting a single sheet of paper. He read it quickly, then slowed down and read it again just to be sure.

There was the usual set of headers identifying the intended recipient and the classification of the message itself. Cade checked to be certain the orders were, indeed, directed at him and then focused on the relevant lines.

> *"The High Command considers the portal to be an unacceptable breach of the integrity of our world. It is to be closed down immediately using any and all means necessary. We see this as the highest priority and destruction of the church is authorized if needed to accomplish this task.*
>
> *Both Delta and Echo are hereby reassigned as adjunct support to the North American Preceptory until the threat of a Chiang Shih incursion has been neutralized."*
>
> *Jacob MacIntyre, Seneschal.*

"Damn it!" Cade turned to hand the letter to Riley and as he did so he caught the smile of satisfaction on the Preceptor's face.

It was too much.

Sergeant Sean Duncan might not have been with Echo for

very long, and he'd certainly had his share of difficulties fitting in with Cade's unorthodox leadership abilities, but there was no doubt in Cade's mind that Duncan was worth ten times what a man like Johannson was.

All three of the other men in Echo command unit owed their lives in one way or another to Sean Duncan.

It had been Duncan who had saved Olsen's life when the chopper they were in had crashed into the Necromancer's plantation house.

It had been Duncan who had worked with Riley and the shade of Cade's dead wife, Gabrielle, to help them escape when the renegade angel Baraquel had forced them into some strange warped version of reality inside the Eden Facility.

Duncan who had used his healing ability to stop Cade's internal bleeding during that same confrontation.

Hell, Olsen had given his life trying to save Duncan's, and abandoning him to the hands of the Chiang Shih repudiated everything that Olsen had died trying to accomplish.

Cade didn't care what his orders said. He was going to rescue Duncan or die trying.

It was simple as that. No pissant little self-important politician was going to stop him.

Riley must have seen the change in Cade's expression for he tried to stop him, moving to put his body between the two men.

"Boss, I don't think…"

But Cade was already in motion. He surged forward, past Riley, grabbing Preceptor Johannson around the throat with one hand and forcing him backward until they crashed into the wall at their backs. Cade leaned in close, his iron grip still locked on the other man's neck, squeezing.

"Listen to me, you pompous son-of-a-bitch!" Cade said in a

grim voice only the two of them could hear. "That man has put his life on the line for this Order more times than I can count and I'll be damned to hell if I simply abandon him because a coward like you ordered me to do so."

The Preceptor had both of his hands on Cade's, trying to break the other man's grip, but was getting nowhere quickly. Cade tightened his fingers slightly, just to show who was in charge.

"The majority of men in this building would rather take orders from me than you any day of the week, so I suggest that you get your sorry ass out of here before I tell them that you just ordered me to abandon one of their own. Understand?"

Johansson's eyes were rolling wildly and his face was turning a deep shade of red as he fought for air, but he must have understood for he managed to nod in agreement. Riley was pulling at Cade's arms now, telling him that it wasn't worth it and that he should let go, and Cade did so.

The Preceptor immediately fell to his knees, his head bowed as he sucked in great gasps of air. When at last he could breathe, he pointed his finger at Cade and, turning to Riley, said shakily, "Master Sergeant, arrest this man for striking a superior officer. Arrest him and throw him in the brig."

Riley looked down at him for a moment and then shrugged.

"Superior officer? I don't think so. If you want him arrested so badly, get up and do it yourself."

And with that the two men from Echo turned away and walked out of the room.

"You've done it now, boss," Riley said, as they walked down the corridor toward the sanctuary proper.

"Screw it. No way am I taking orders from that stupid son-of-a-bitch. We've got to go after Duncan and we've got to do it now."

"Agreed. So how do you want to handle things?"

Cade stopped and gave it a moment's thought. "Who do we have with us, right now?"

"First and Second Squad, minus Jones, Santiago, and, well, you know."

Riley couldn't bring himself to say the dead man's name and Cade didn't blame him. Echo just wouldn't be the same without Olsen.

"Third Squad?"

"Won't be here until later tonight. They were in the midst of an exercise in the Sierra Madres when the call came down. Denton got them underway as soon as possible but it still takes time to get a group of that size halfway across the country."

"All right, we'll have to make do with who we've got. Assemble the men in the sanctuary in fifteen minutes. I'll address them there."

* * *

"So that's where things stand. I'm sure Johannson will have both myself and Master Sergeant Riley up on charges before the hour is out. I'll happily submit myself to face those charges, too, but not until I've tried to rescue Sergeant Duncan."

Cade stopped and looked out over the men assembled in the front pews before him. They were good men, all of them, but what he was asking them to do went against everything a professional soldier stood for. Chain of command was the backbone of any professional fighting force and to blatantly forgo it as he was asking them to do was, well, asking a lot. Still, no one had gotten up and walked out, so he took that as a good sign and went on.

"It's my intention to mount a raid against the Chiang Shih encampment and rescue Sergeant Duncan. I'll not leave one of my men in the hands of those vile things and a rapid strike seems to have the best chance of succeeding.

"Understand that this is strictly a volunteer operation. Anyone choosing to accompany me will more than likely face charges of insubordination and disobeying a direct order, never mind mounting an illegal and unsanctioned operation. Nor can we expect back-up should anything go wrong and I'm sure I don't need to remind any of you how often that can happen. Our previous excursion is a perfect example.

"Still, Master Sergeant Riley and I can't do this alone. We need all of the help we can get. So we're going to step outside of the room, give you a chance to talk this over amongst yourselves. There is no shame in choosing to stay behind. After all, I am asking you to follow an illegal order. All I ask is that you give us enough time to make the crossing before reporting our departure to the authorities at Ravensgate."

Cade glanced over at Riley, to be certain he hadn't missed anything, and at the slight nod of the other man's head, he wrapped it up.

"So talk it over. Make your decision with your head, as well as your heart. I'll see you in a moment."

Cade stepped down from the altar steps, heading for the door leading to the hallway with Riley at his side when someone called his name.

He turned to find the entire contingent of men on their feet. Sergeant Davis from First Squad had come out of the pews to stand in front of them.

"I think I speak for all of us, sir, when I tell you that there is

131

no need for further discussion," said Davis. "We'll follow you wherever you ask us to go. In this world or the next."

He snapped to attention and behind him each and every one of the other soldiers did the same.

Cade looked over at Riley, who grinned back and said, "Looks like you've got yourself a strike team, Commander. Let's go get our man."

CHAPTER 21

"A CAPTIVE OF THE ENEMY"

A BUCKET OF ICE-COLD WATER was thrown in his face and Duncan awoke, spluttering. When he could breathe again he realized that he was now hanging upside down, his wrists and ankles bound with thick chains, the slack between his legs slung around a hook protruding from the ceiling, leaving him trussed up like a side of beef ready for curing.

He tried to raise his head, wanting a better look at the chains that held him, but even that slight movement brought a wave of overwhelming pain, forcing him to relax lest he pass out again.

He was naked, that much he knew. The air around him was cold and clammy on his bruised and battered body. His vision was limited, his left eye swollen nearly shut, and his lips stung where they had cracked and split open. The cut on his forehead, though not deep, throbbed in time with the beat of his heart, as did the knife wound in his shoulder. The latter, at least, had stopped bleeding. His arms dangled down over his head, his fingertips just barely touching the floor, but the hours he'd spent chained up had robbed him of any feeling in them.

The pain was good.

He welcomed it, basked in its presence, for it let him know he was still alive. And every moment he lived and breathed was another moment in which he might be rescued.

The Order would come for him, he was sure of it.

He clung to the notion the way a drowning swimmer will cling to an errant piece of wreckage, steadfast in his belief. To allow any other consideration to enter his thoughts would bring doubt. Close on doubt's heels lurked despair and he knew that to succumb to despair in this place would be the beginning of the end.

He had to stay strong, had to believe that Cade and the others would come for him. It was just a matter of time, he told himself, just a matter of time. Hang in there.

A foot shuffled nearby and dragged him back to the here and now. Out of the corner of his eye he could see one of his jailers standing there, waiting. Duncan soon found out for what.

With a clank of bolts being withdrawn, a door on the other side of the room opened and Bishop walked in.

The very sight of him set Duncan's body twitching involuntarily. His mind might still be his own but Duncan knew that his body had betrayed him sometime earlier. Hours of pain at this man's hands had instilled in him a conditioned set of reactions. He could feel his heart rate accelerating and his bladder threatened to let go against his will. The mind rebelled but the flesh remembered.

The flesh remembered.

He had to hold out, had to give Cade and the others time to

get here.

It wouldn't be much longer.

Couldn't be much longer.

Bishop crossed the room and squatted in front of him. As if he were reading his mind, Bishop smiled and said, "They're not coming for you, you know."

Duncan looked away, saying nothing.

"Whether you want to admit it or not, you're on your own. They won't risk the entire squad just to rescue one man."

Duncan focused on a patch of nearby wall, refusing to acknowledge what the other was saying.

"It makes no tactical sense. You know it as well as I do. Cade won't risk the others. Not to rescue someone like you. The new guy. The guy who hasn't even been a member of the team long enough to matter."

That last comment broke Duncan's carefully manufactured façade. Anger flared somewhere inside.

"Shut the hell up, asshole."

He regretted the comment the moment it left his lips.

Bishop simply nodded in disappointment. "Don't you know? I'm well acquainted with our dear friend Cade Williams."

Like a cat playing with its food, Bishop reached up and began prodding Duncan's body, each jab sending waves of agony washing over him. Duncan clamped his mouth shut, refusing to cry out.

"He's not coming."

"I should know."

"Once, I was in the same position as you are; lost, trapped, beaten and bruised but refusing to give up my companions, trusting that they would return and rescue me from the hell in which I found myself. And do you know what happened?"

Duncan steadfastly refused to make a sound.

Quick as a snake, Bishop's hand shot out and grasped Duncan's wounded shoulder, squeezing it viciously.

The pain was excruciating.

Duncan screamed.

Bishop shouted over him, wanting to be sure Duncan heard him beyond his pain. "He left me there, lost and alone, at the mercy of my captors! Abandoned by the one man who could have rescued me. Just as surely as he's abandoned you!"

Bishop let go, turning away in disgust.

Gasping, Duncan fought to keep from blacking out. He was dimly aware of the door opening, but the pain kept him from giving it his full attention. It was only when the tramp of booted feet intruded on his consciousness that he forced his eyes open to see what new pleasures Bishop had in store for him.

Three other Chiang Shih had entered the room, including the hulking brute who had beaten Duncan senseless the night before, but the sight of them didn't bother the captive at all. He was too focused on the four humans who followed in their wake. Dirty, disheveled, sporting fresh set bruises of their own, still Duncan recognized them as the three priests and the young nun who had spoken with him and Cade several days before. Seeing them, Duncan was embarrassed by his nakedness, but there wasn't much he could do about it so he tried to put it out of his head.

Bishop said something in a language Duncan didn't understand and the three Chiang Shih moved toward him.

Bracing himself for another beating, Duncan was surprised when they lifted him up, freed the chain from the hook above and set him down on his feet, unharmed. His legs couldn't hold him and he collapsed to the cold stone floor. The brute hissed in annoyance and hauled Duncan back up to his knees, forcing him to kneel. To be certain he didn't collapse a second time, the creature kept his hand firmly locked on the top of Duncan's skull, holding him upright.

Another command from Bishop and the four captives were then hauled forward and forced to their knees, facing Duncan with only a few feet separating them. Duncan could see the pain and terror in their eyes, could hear their unspoken pleas for him to do something, anything, to get them away from these monsters.

Bishop stalked forward until he stood behind the first of the captives and stared down at Duncan.

After a long silence, broken only by the nun's quiet weeping, Bishop reached out and placed his clawed hands on either side of the priest's head.

"All right," he said softly, "time for a few simple questions. If you tell me what I want to know, I'll let these people go."

Bishop smiled, a sudden, predatory smile full of teeth. "Tell me the make-up and armament of all the Templar units now within the city limits."

Duncan stared directly into Bishop's yellow eyes. Slowly he shook his head and repeated his answer from earlier.

"I can't tell you that."

Bishop shrugged.

"Okay, have it your way."

With a quick snap of his wrists, he broke the priest's neck and then stepped back, watching as the body crashed to the floor, the man's sightless eyes staring into eternity.

Bishop stepped over to the next man in line.

"No, please," the priest whimpered, leaning forward in a vain attempt to stay out of reach, but Bishop just laughed, grabbed the man's hair, and hauled him upward. He leaned down, his tongue flicking out and caressing the edge of the man's ear.

The hot stink of excrement filled the room and the man's face went slack with fear.

Duncan felt sorry for him, but there wasn't anything he could do to save him. There was no way he was giving up Echo or any of the other strike teams in the vicinity. Doing so would leave the entire populace of Boston at the Chiang Shih's hands, for with the information Bishop wanted he could wipe out all of the strike teams before they could even be brought to bear against the threat.

No, the priest was a man of God. He of all people should understand the reward waiting for him in heaven, should know that his life here on earth was being exchanged for something far better.

They were both soldiers in Christ; there wasn't any choice to be made.

Bishop repeated his question.

Without taking his gaze off the face of the man before him, Duncan shook his head.

This time Bishop wasn't as gentle. He grabbed the man's head between his hands and wrenched it savagely to the side, twisting it until the flesh of the neck ripped apart and the head came free. Blood spurted upward, splashing across Bishop's dark coat, as well as the face of the priest kneeling next in line.

Bishop cast the man's decapitated head aside and Duncan was certain he would remember the odd thumping sound it made as it skipped across the stone floor and out of sight somewhere behind him for the rest of his life. He said a prayer for the man's soul and then added one for his own.

When he looked up he found Bishop watching him closely. The man's eyes narrowed and he looked to the two remaining prisoners, then back at Duncan before seeming to come to a decision. He barked out another command.

The Chiang Shih soldiers stepped up, unchained the remaining priest, and dragged him away from the nun. As Duncan looked on they forced him to lie flat on the floor and held him down with arms and legs extended. The priest had his eyes squeezed shut and was praying aloud the entire time, stopping only when one of the Chiang Shih cuffed him on the side of the head.

Bishop knelt down in front of Duncan so that they were eye to eye. "You're a soldier. Death doesn't scare you. I can understand that. And I can also understand your willingness to let your fellow captives give their lives in order to protect those you consider friends. After all, what are they to you?"

His reasoning was off, but Duncan wasn't about to correct him. He knew it didn't matter what the vile thing in front of him believed. God would understand the reasoning.

But Bishop wasn't finished.

"There are things worse than death, however, as I'm sure you understand Sergeant Duncan." He drew out the name, mocking him. "Things that would make a good little knight like you recoil in horror and disgust. Things to damn your soul for all eternity."

He stalked over to where his companions held the prisoner to the floor. "Can you justify your silence in the face of something like that? Can you hold your tongue, knowing your silence can send another to the bottomless pit, their link to the divine forever severed?"

He straddled the priest, putting one knee on either side of the man's chest, and glanced once more at Duncan. "Let's just see, shall we?"

The priest began twisting and turning his head, trying to keep it free, but Bishop grabbed it with both hands and held it steady against the man's struggles. Bending down, Bishop forced his lips over the other man's, as if he was going to give him mouth-to-mouth resuscitation, but rather than breathing out, Bishop breathed in.

The priest's eyes widened and then his body bucked upward spasmodically, once, twice, three times. Bishop rode them out like a cowboy on a bronco, as if he'd done this a thousand times before, and after the third spasm the priest went limp.

Bishop gave a small grunt of pleasure and began to work at his victim, sucking at his face, his cheeks puffing in and out furiously as he dragged something free of the priest's body. An odd slurping sound filled the room. For Duncan's benefit he pulled back slightly, revealing the prize he sought.

A luminescent, mist-like substance was being pulled from deep inside the priest, flowing out from his mouth, across the space between the two men, and into Bishop's gaping maw. The Chiang Shih commander drank it down greedily, his chest and shoulder's heaving as he worked to bring as much of it up as possible. In contrast the priest's body began to shrink in upon itself, the flesh turning a slate grey while shriveling up like a dried piece of fruit as Bishop sucked more and more of the man's life force out of his form.

It went on far longer than Duncan could bear to watch. He squeezed his eyes shut and turned away, praying for the man's soul.

At last the slurping sound stopped.

When Duncan opened his eyes, he found Bishop squatting a few feet away, an amused smile on his face. Behind him, the desiccated body of the priest lay on the stone floor, discarded like so much trash.

Duncan faced his tormentor defiantly, both for himself and the dead man on the floor before him. "You can do whatever you want to our bodies, but our souls belong to God and nothing you can do can separate us from Him. Killing us only hastens our entrance into heaven."

Bishop laughed in his face.

Movement caught Duncan's attention.

A sudden, unexplained dread stole over him as he turned to get a better look.

On the ground behind Bishop, the man Duncan had assumed was dead slowly turned his head.

Their eyes met.

The priest's groan of horror almost drowned out Duncan's own.

Unable to look, Duncan tried to turn away, but Bishop wouldn't let him. He grabbed Duncan and forced him to face the last of the four prisoners, the young nun.

"Look at her!" he commanded.

Duncan did. She was young, in her late twenties, thirty at most, with curly brown hair. Her blue eyes blazed in sharp contrast to the greyness all around them.

"Don't tell him anything," she said in a trembling voice, holding Duncan's gaze, doing what she could to put on a brave show.

But all the Templar sergeant could see was an image of her face, sunken in on itself, horribly transformed like the priest's as the very life force within her was sucked up to satisfy the ravenous hunger of the vile creature standing nearby. There was no way he could watch this innocent young woman suffer like that, particularly when he considered the spiritual ramifications of the act. To have one's soul forever trapped like that, cut off from God? Damn the consequences, but he couldn't do it. The moans of pain and horror still issuing from the shadows in the corner only helped confirm his decision.

Enough was enough.

When Bishop quietly began asking questions a moment later, Duncan told him what he wanted to know.

CHAPTER 22

"MONSTROUS REVELATIONS"

VOICES INTRUDED, BROUGHT HIM BACK from the darkness into the light.

Duncan lay still, listening, not wanting to give away the fact that he was awake until he could get his bearings and figure out what was going on.

After he revealed what he knew to Bishop, he was emotionally and physically exhausted. That hadn't stopped his captors from beating him practically senseless again. He had vague memories of being dragged out of the ruined building, across the rocky ground, and into one of the tents set up on the plain. At that point he'd finally lapsed into unconsciousness and had no idea how long he'd been out.

The voices were close, but didn't sound as if they were in the same room, and so he decided to take a chance. His left eye was still swollen shut, but his right worked and by cracking it slightly he was able to get a limited view of the room without, he hoped, revealing to anyone that might be watching that he was awake and aware.

.He lay on a dirt floor. That much was immediately obvious from the dirt and rock directly in front of his face. From the lack of feeling in his hands and feet he knew he was trussed up like a Christmas turkey. He turned his head slightly and as his eyesight adjusted to the dim light, he was able to make out a bit more. His memory of the tent was correct; he lay inside a large structure made of canvas or some similar material, supported on a framework of thick wooden posts. The room he lay in was separated from another by a large piece of cloth. A thin strip of light revealed where the gap hadn't been closed completely.

The voices, one male, one female, were coming from the other side of the partition and he could make out the silhouette of the man against the fabric, pacing back and forth as he spoke.

Duncan sensed that what was going on in the next room was important, not just for him but for the fate of those on the other side of the Veil, and he knew he had to get a look at whoever was in there. His position on the floor didn't allow him to see through the gap in the partition, however, and he knew he'd have to move to manage it.

He slowly rolled over, ignoring the sharp jab of a rock that cut into his already bruised flesh and then, seeing it wasn't enough, did it again one more time. That did the trick. Now he could see through the slight gap into the room beyond and he got his first look at the female speaker.

She was a stunningly beautiful Asian woman with a finely featured face, large eyes, and hair the color of midnight that stretched down past her waist in a long flowing wave. Dressed in traditional Japanese attire, she lounged on a throne made from some kind of black material. Obsidian, maybe. She held an intricately decorated paper fan in one hand, her long nails painted crimson and sheathed in gold, and she waved the fan around as if in punctuation to what she was saying.

"You are certain this will work?"

"Most definitely, Princess. He will return for his teammate, just as he once tried to return for me. At that point he will be at the mercy of our soldiers."

Duncan couldn't see whom she was speaking to but the voice that responded was unmistakably male, with the slightest hint of an accent, and he had little doubt that the man was Bishop.

"I'll be quite displeased if things do not go as you foresee."

The steel in her voice made it clear she was used to being obeyed.

Bishop, however, didn't sound concerned in the slightest.

"Have no fear, my lady. Things have gone exactly as we've planned and the information given to me by our captive will certainly give us an edge on our opposition. When that bastard Templar and his men cross the Veil, we will be more than prepared to deal with them in the manner they deserve."

Bishop chuckled. "By battle's end, the ranks of your soldiers should have swelled appreciatively. And this time, they will come with more than their fair share of combat experience."

Good Lord! The entire situation had been manufactured to draw Cade and the rest of the Templar fighting elite into a trap. He had to get out free and warn them before it was too late. But how?

Confident now that he was alone, he turned his head and took in the rest of the room. He could see that the lower edge of the tent had been spiked to the ground every couple of feet. Even if he could get free of his bonds, there was no way he could fit between the gaps. No, if he was going to get out, he would have to either cut through the fabric itself or make his way into the next room and fight his way out through the front entrance.

He didn't imagine he'd be able to cut through the tent wall with his teeth, his knife long since having been taken from him, which meant the later was his only option.

Obviously not the best of plans, but it would have to do.

First things first, though. He had to get out of these bonds.

But even as he began to twist and turn his wrists, trying to loosen his bindings, the conversation in the next room caught his attention.

"Remember our agreement. Once we lure the Templars here, Commander Williams is mine. The Master expects me to deliver him intact and we don't want to disappoint him."

The Princess laughed dismissively. "I'd deliver that renegade from Hell a hundred such souls if it will help him keep his side of the bargain and shatter the Veil as he claims."

"Good. Then we're in agreement and all that's left is to bait the trap."

"Which will happen when?"

"Soon. Very soon. The last of my troops are moving into position as we speak and it should only take the witches another hour or so to prepare the Curtain around our positions. After that, all we have left to do is sit back and wait. When our righteous little friends launch their operation against us, they'll find that we have more than one trick up our sleeves."

Their laughter filled the room and Duncan knew that there was far more to this than Cade suspected. The Chiang Shih weren't just planning an incursion into the living world, but apparently had struck some kind of deal with a more powerful force to shatter the barrier between the worlds themselves. He didn't know much about the Beyond, but what he did know made him absolutely certain that destroying the Veil was a very bad idea.

Think, Duncan, think!

He knew his time was rapidly running out. But so far his bonds had resisted his attempts to loosen them and he didn't think he had the energy left to keep working at them with brute strength alone. If he was going to get free in time to make a difference, he had to find a better way.

He shifted position and the sudden spike of resulting pain let him know that he had at least one, maybe two, broken ribs to go along with the festering knife wound in his shoulder. A lot of good he was going to be in a fight.

The pain in his ribs reminded him of the rock he'd rolled over a few minutes before and a plan blossomed in his mind. Now if the damn thing was only sharp enough...

He rolled back in the direction he'd started from, until a jab in his back let him know he'd found what he was looking for. As quietly as possible he maneuvered himself around until he could feel the sharp edges of the rock with his fingers. Taking it in hand, he began to saw it back and forth against the bonds that held him.

It was slow work. The rope was tight and allowed very limited movement. The lack of feeling in his fingers made it hard for him to position the stone properly. More than once he sliced through his fingers or the flesh of his wrist and the rock began to get slippery with his blood, making it even harder to hold.

At this rate I'm going to bleed to death before I get out of here, he thought, but he didn't stop.

It might have been an hour, maybe more, his sense of time having long since fled, but eventually he felt his bonds grow looser and knew he'd managed to cut through the first strand of rope.

Invigorated by his success, he set to with a renewed sense of urgency.

Light flooded the room behind him and Bishop's voice rang out.

"What's this? Our guest has had enough of our hospitality?"

Footsteps crossed the room as Duncan cursed inwardly. *He was so damned close!*

He looked up to find Bishop standing over him, a cruel smile playing across the man's face.

Without another word the Chiang Shih commander lifted a booted foot and brought it down viciously against Duncan's temple.

The room went dark and the youngest member of the Echo Team knew no more.

CHAPTER 23

"UNVEILED"

RILEY HANDED CADE THE BINOCULARS. "He's about three hundred yards west of us, down on the plain. Looks like they beat feet and left him behind."

After the decision to defy the Seneschal's orders, Cade and his men had wasted little time in replenishing their supplies and returning to the Beyond. They made the trek to the Chiang Shih camp as swiftly as possible, knowing that every second spent in their world might have translated into hours on the other side of reality.

Now it looked like they might be too late.

From their vantage point on the ridge, they could see that the tents that had housed the Chiang Shih still littered the plain, but rather than being filled with the teeming horde they'd expected they now appeared to be deserted. Several of them had been partially dismantled, as if the owners had been forced to flee in the midst of the job. The great bonfires that had marked the encampment when the Templars had last seen it were now nothing more than piles of black ash, though several still gave off thin wisps of smoke that climbed into the sky like disembodied spirits, indicating it hadn't been all that long since they'd been doused.

In the middle of it all was Duncan. He was tied upright to a thick post that had been driven into the earth beneath his feet and even at this distance Cade could see the terrible bruises that covered the young Templar's face. He hung against the ropes that bound him to the post, unmoving, and Cade couldn't be sure if he was alive.

Nor did he dare use his Sight to find out. Doing so would attract the attention of other denizens of the Beyond and they didn't need any additional foes to worry about.

No, they were going to have to do this the old fashioned way. They had to go and see for themselves.

A bit of searching revealed a narrow trail and the team carefully picked their way down to the plain below. From there they made a cautious approach, using what cover they could find, until they reached the edge of the encampment. There, Cade called a halt.

"What do you think?" he asked his executive officer.

Riley gazed out over the abandoned encampment for a long moment and then, "They're out there. Somewhere. I can feel them."

The other man nodded. "Yeah. Me, too. But we expected that. What I need to know is if we risk it?"

Riley turned toward him. "We don't really have a choice, do we?" he asked, and Cade had to agree.

They didn't have a choice. They'd come here to rescue Duncan and the only way to do that was to stroll right through the enemy's camp and untie him from that pole. Anything else was just an obstacle they had to face in order to accomplish their mission.

Riley passed the word and the men formed up around Cade. They would enter the encampment and form a defensive perimeter around the pole while Cade checked on their teammate. If he was still alive, Cade would cut him down and they would retreat as expeditiously as possible. If something went wrong, if they were attacked or got separated, they agreed to regroup at the portal where they could return to their side of reality.

Satisfied with the arrangements, Cade gave the order and the team moved out.

The center of the encampment where Duncan was being held hostage was only two hundred yards away, but to Cade it felt like two miles. Every step brought them deeper into the heart of the enemy's camp and while he couldn't see them, Cade knew they were out there. Somewhere. He could feel it in his bones and crawling across his skin, that sense that a hundred pairs of eyes were watching his every move, and his body was tense with anticipation, waiting for the sudden attack.

Much to his surprise, it didn't come and they were able to reach Duncan without incident.

As the others took their places, Cade moved the last few yards and reached out for their fallen comrade.

He was acutely aware that Duncan's position carefully mimicked that in which he'd found Bishop on that fateful day several years before, and recognized it for the message that it was. Bishop wanted him to know that he still remembered that day, too, and it was clear that he blamed Cade for his current state of existence. They were on opposite sides of right and wrong and Cade had no choice but to stop his former teammate before more harm was done.

Reaching out, he gently lifted Duncan's head.

He'd been beaten more than once, the older bruises having already turned a deep purple in color while the newer ones were doing their best to catch up. One eye was swollen completely shut, his lips split in several places, and his open mouth revealed that he was going to need several courses of reconstructive surgery if he ever wanted to smile again.

To Cade's surprise, not only was the other man alive, but he was conscious as well.

Duncan opened one eye and said something too soft for Cade to hear.

He bent closer. "What was that, Duncan?"

"It's a trap."

Cade pulled back so Duncan could see his face, a grim smile dancing at the corners of his mouth. "I know."

"But..."

"Quiet. Let me worry about that. You just hold yourself together until we can get you back to a hospital on the other side. Brace yourself, because I'm going to cut your down."

Cade pulled his knife and, positioning himself in front of Duncan, cut the ropes that bound him to the post. Duncan slumped forward, unable to support his own weight, and Cade caught him gently in his arms. Knowing time was of the essence, he hefted Duncan over his shoulder and turned, intent on getting him and the rest of his team out as quickly as possible.

The Chiang Shih chose that moment to reveal themselves.

At a shouted command from Bishop, the enemy mystics dropped the illusion they had been using to hide their presence. Echo suddenly found itself surrounded by the missing horde.

152

They were everywhere.

Packed into the narrow spaces between the tents, standing inside the structures themselves, even blocking the pathway the knights had just taken through the camp to reach Duncan. As the two groups stared at each other, a single Chiang Shih stepped forward.

He was tall and muscular, with blonde hair and blue eyes, the kind of man that most women would find instantly attractive, if it hadn't been for the cruel set of his features or the hard gleam of hatred in his eyes.

Cade was not surprised to see him.

"Hello Bishop," he said calmly.

He'd suspected the other's presence ever since they'd discovered the Chiang Shih encampment, but having it confirmed didn't give him any sense of satisfaction. Bishop had been a good man, a good knight, and to see him reduced to his present condition was a vivid reminder that Cade had failed him all those years before and had continued to fail him every day since.

"Commander." The other man's voice dripped with sarcasm and it was clear to Cade that he didn't feel Cade was truly in command of anything at this point.

Cade didn't blame him; what commander worth his salt would lead his men intentionally into a trap like this? But Cade never did things without a reason. He still had one more card to throw and it was time to see if Bishop would play along.

"What do you want, Bishop?"

The former Templar soldier laughed. There was very little trace of his humanity left in that laugh. "What do I want? I would have thought that would be obvious at this point, Williams. Would it be too cliché if I said I wanted you dead?"

Cade shrugged. "Originality was never your strong suit."

"Go ahead and make jokes. They don't bother me. You'll still scream just as loudly in the end."

Out of the corner of his eye Cade could see Riley and several of the others shifting position, readying themselves for a final fatal charge against the vile creatures surrounding them.

"Hold!" he said sharply.

Riley shot him a look but obeyed just the same, for which Cade was thankful. As long as Riley held steady, the others would as well.

Bishop glanced over to see who Cade was speaking to and his smile grew wider, if that was at all possible. "My, my, my. If it isn't my old teammate Sergeant Riley. Still taking orders from your betters?"

Riley ignored him.

"No matter. You've simply saved me the trouble of hunting you down and killing you separately. I guess I should be thankful for that."

The Chiang Shih around them laughed in appreciation at Bishop's joke and the sound made Cade's skin crawl.

"If it's my death you want, Bishop, then let's make a deal."

"A deal? What do I need a deal for? All I have to do is give the word and you'll be dead in seconds."

"But then you won't have the pleasure of killing me yourself. Where's the fun in that?" Now it was Cade's turn to smile. "Unless you're afraid to face me again? After all, I did kill you the last time we faced each other."

Bishop stalked forward, suddenly furious. "I'll kill you now, you stupid little…"

"You'll do no such thing."

The newcomer's voice rang with the iron tone of command

and it pulled Bishop up short. Cade watched in amazement as the crowd parted behind the former knight, revealing the speaker.

In her human guise she was beautiful, a tall, lithe woman of Asian descent with porcelain skin and long dark hair the color of crow feathers, the kind of woman men would fight over, but Cade didn't need his special sight to know that beneath that casual façade lingered a slavering beast that would feast on him as readily as her lieutenant would. She was surrounded by some of the largest Chiang Shih Cade had ever seen, obviously bodyguards, and the way Bishop deferred to her made Cade realize where the true power was.

"Princess," Bishop said stiffly. "This is no concern of yours."

"But it is, Bishop, it is. After all, I can't have anyone, least of all a mere human, casting doubt on my lieutenant's abilities, can I?"

Bishop waved her concerns away. "Williams has been promised to another or have you forgotten our agreement?"

The woman laughed, a cruel, dismissive sound and Cade had the sense that she had seized on the situation to show the others just who was in charge here. Her response only served to confirm his suspicions.

"I made no such agreement, Bishop. That was you and you alone. How you honor that agreement is your business, not mine."

Bishop snarled in frustration, but didn't argue with her any further.

Apparently the woman, *the Princess*, Cade corrected himself, was satisfied with that, for she moved past Bishop without another word and stepped up in front of Cade, extending her hand.

"I am Princess Akiko."

Cade nodded, acknowledging her introduction, but refusing to take her hand.

She ignored the slight and looked him for several long minutes. "We have met once before, haven't we?" she asked finally.

Cade nodded. "Yes."

"Then you know who I am."

Again Cade nodded, but didn't tell her that it had nothing to do with their prior confrontation. The Order maintained extensive files on all manner of supernatural creatures and the Chiang Shih were no exception. Much like the way in which the police traced the connections among the major crime families that once ruled New York, Chicago, and Philadelphia, so, too, did the Order track their enemies in a similar manner. Cade knew that Akiko was a minor member of one of the Chiang Shih's ruling bloodlines. As such, he never would have expected her of being the power behind such a large war force. There was obviously more going on here than he knew.

"Good. I'll accept your challenge."

"I'm sorry?" said Cade, misunderstanding.

"Single combat. You against Bishop. If you lose, the lives of your men are also forfeit."

"And if I win?"

She smiled and Cade caught the gleam of teeth that had been filed to a point. "Then I will allow you and your men a head start before I release the rest of my hunters on your trail."

It was the best he was going to get and Cade knew it. At the very least, it gave his men a fighting chance. It would also give him time to figure out just what "agreement" Bishop was talking about.

"With a deal like that, and the odds so overwhelmingly on my side, how could I say no?" he replied.

The Princess clapped her hands together like a little girl and laughed in delight. "You amuse me, Commander Cade Williams. When Bishop is done with you, perhaps I will take you into my house as my servant. Would you like that?"

"You have far too much confidence in your champion, my lady."

"We shall see, Commander, we shall see. You will have five minutes to confer with your men and then the battle shall begin."

And with that she turned away and began giving orders to her warriors, preparing for the confrontation to come.

CHAPTER 24

"FACE OFF"

B Y SHEER FORCE OF NUMBERS, the Chiang Shih herded the men of Echo to the far side of the camp, where a large circular ring was already laid out on the ground in front of a wooden platform that reminded Cade of an improvised stage. The sides of the circle were of piled stone and the center was full of sand. Apparently this was where he was to fight Bishop, and if the stains on the ground were any indication, it wouldn't be the first fight to the death that had been held here. As the Chiang Shih began preparing for the confrontation, Cade joined the rest of his men off to one side of the gathering crowd.

Duncan was stretched out unconscious on the ground and Davis was kneeling beside him, using his med kit to tend to the other man's wounds.

"How is he?" Cade asked.

Davis looked up. "Better than I expected. He's got at least a couple of broken ribs and possibly a concussion, though I can't be certain of the later without further testing. They beat him and cut him up pretty badly, but whoever did it knew what they were doing. He won't ever look the same, but nothing they did is life threatening. With time, and plenty of rest, he should do all right."

"Good. Keep him comfortable and be ready to move quickly if we get the chance."

"Roger that."

Cade said a few words to the rest of the men, reassuring them with the calm confidence in his voice and his generally upbeat tone, and by the time he turned away to speak to Riley a few of them were even smiling in his wake.

The Knight Commander stepped over to where Riley stood guard at the edge of the circle, glaring at those Chiang Shih that wandered a bit too close. He handed his sword to him and then shed his body armor, piece by piece. Cade knew that he needed to be quick on his feet and while the heavy tactical suit might protect him from more than just a glancing blow, it would also limit his movements and slow him considerably. He quickly stripped off his shirt as well, not wanting Bishop to be able to use it as leverage against him should the fighting get in close and dirty. He considered discarding his boots, but ultimately decided against it. He'd learned long ago that on uncertain ground bare feet were best, but in this case he'd trade that stability for the additional damage the heavy boots would add to any strike he might deliver with them.

Satisfied with his preparations, he turned back to Riley and drew his sword from the scabbard in the other man's hands. As he did so, Cade passed a few last minute instructions to his executive officer.

"You know you can't trust her, right?"

Riley grunted. "Of course not." He kept his attention on those around them, just as Cade was doing, wary that one of the Chiang Shih might use a momentary lack of attention to attack despite Princess Akiko's orders.

"Good. And you and I both know that Johannson won't be sending anyone after us, especially after I disobeyed his direct order. So we're on our own."

"What else is new?" Riley said, in his typical dour style.

Cade had to chuckle at that and was suddenly glad that he had the big master sergeant at his side. The two of them had been through a lot in their years together and he wouldn't want any other man beside him at a time like this. He knew he could trust Riley to do the right thing when the time came.

"I don't see a way out of this yet, but the day's still young. Keep your eyes open and if you have a chance to save the rest of the team out of here, don't hesitate to take it."

"Roger that."

Cade looked at him and could see that despite his agreement, Riley had no intention of leaving him behind no matter what opportunity might present itself. Cade didn't blame him; if their position had been reversed he wouldn't do it either. They'd returned to the Beyond to rescue a missing teammate; there was no way either of them would leave the other behind at this point.

Riley met his gaze and in the other man's eyes Cade could see all the things that he wanted to say as well, things that would never be voiced but that both men understood, nevertheless. Cade nodded in understanding and slapped him on the shoulder, knowing that nothing further needed to be said.

He turned and looked out over the makeshift arena before them, gauging the amount of space available, making note of the places where the ground was uneven and where it was smooth.

He had no doubt that Bishop would be a dangerous opponent, for on top of his Templar training the other man could now add inhuman strength and speed to his arsenal. Cade knew he was going to need every advantage that he could get in order to come out on top. He was confident that he was the better technical swordsman, but if it came to a hand-to-hand brawl dependent on speed and stamina he was going to be seriously outclassed.

A commotion caught his attention and he turned in time to see Princess Akiko being led through the crowd. The throne on which she rode was heavy enough that it took eight men to carry it and was made of a stone so black that seemed to suck the light right out of the space around her. For all Cade knew, maybe it actually did.

The throne was carried up onto the platform and set down near the edge. The princess stood and gestured off to one side. In response the crowd parted and Bishop strode forward. He stopped before the platform and received a few words of encouragement or strategy from the princess, then joined Cade in the center of the circle.

As he approached, Cade settled into his combat stance, not wanting to be caught unprepared should things start suddenly. He stood with his left foot ahead of his right, with his body turned slightly to the side to present a slimmer target for his foe. He held his sword before him in a two-handed grip, its point directed at Bishop's head. He concentrated on his breathing, knowing he was going to have to win quickly and decisively if he hoped to get out of this alive and the best chance he had to do that was to stay focused and steady.

"You look a bit nervous, Williams," Bishop said in a voice loud enough to carry outside the circle. "Don't worry, I'll make it quick."

The spectators, including the princess, laughed appreciatively.

Cade didn't reply, not wanting to waste even the slightest bit of energy. He would need all he had to win this fight.

Princess Akiko raised her arms and the crowd grew silent. When she was satisfied she faced the crowd and her voice rose over them. "A challenge has been made and accepted. Two shall enter the Circle of Judgment but only one shall prevail and leave its confines."

Her words had the ring of ritual to them and Cade tuned them out. He watched his opponent instead. Bishop stared back, a haughty smile of superiority on his face. Unlike Cade, whose weapon harkened back to the styles used by the Templars in the early days of the Order, Bishop held a Japanese katana and from the way he was rotating it in his one handed grip, it was clear that he was quite comfortable using it. Cade had no doubt the weapon was razor sharp and he made a mental note to be twice as careful. Even a light slash could cause serious damage if he was unlucky enough to get hit.

The princess had finally finished her speech and was returning to her chair. Cade cast one last glance over at Riley, caught a nod of support from the other man, and then turned his attention back to his opponent.

It was do or die time.

The princess clapped her hands and the fight was underway.

Cade began circling to his left, watching Bishop closely, searching for some opening in his guard that he might exploit when the opportunity presented itself.

The other man had no intention of waiting, however.

Bishop exploded toward him, his weapon swinging in toward Cade's midsection in a vicious strike, and the former Templar soldier was even faster than Cade had anticipated.

Cade dropped the point of his sword and met Bishop's blade with the edge of his own, channeling the energy of his attacker's strike away from him and toward the ground instead. He twisted and brought his own weapon up in a semi-circular motion that brought it swinging back in toward Bishop's neck, hoping for a lucky strike to end it all before it had barely begun.

But Bishop was too good to be taken out quickly and he easily blocked Cade's strike in turn.

Back and forth they went, blow after blow, twisting and turning, moving about inside the confines of the circle, each man striving to gain the upper hand to deliver the killing stroke.

It was Bishop who drew first blood, cutting in beneath Cade's guard and slashing the tip of his sword across the knight commander's thigh. Blood flowed, staining Cade's pant leg, and Bishop grinned in triumph.

"I'll carve you up one cut at a time, Commander," he sneered.

Cade ignored him and the cut as well. He could tell it wasn't too deep and he therefore wasn't in any real danger, but still, eventually the blood loss would take its toll he knew.

He'd just have to redouble his efforts and put an end to this before that happened.

Bishop came at him again and they traded another series of blows. The crowd around them was rowdy, shouting and jeering, and Cade tuned them out, focusing on the task at hand.

Wounding Cade made Bishop cocky and his strikes began to get a bit sloppy, his overconfidence working against him. Cade pretended not to notice, slowing down his responses to Bishop's attacks so that it seemed as if he were injured more than he actually was, drawing the other man in closer and closer with every exchange of blows.

Predictably, Bishop closed in, sensing a possible chance at victory.

Which was just what Cade wanted. Bishop was just a hair too slow in recovering from a particularly vicious strike and Cade saw his chance.

He didn't hesitate.

As Bishop came in, Cade feinted to the left and then spun in the opposite direction, coming in under Bishop's guard. The other man was already dropping his elbows down, intending to hammer Cade's weapon into the dirt with the force of the blow before it could reach him, but the sword strike was simply another distraction. Cade's real attack came from a completely unexpected direction as he lifted his right leg and slammed his booted foot down on the inside of Bishop's knee.

There was a sharp crack, heard even over the shouts of the crowd, and the knee gave way, dropping his opponent to the ground on one leg.

As a result Bishop's counter strike missed and his neck was suddenly at the same level as Cade's slashing weapon.

Another few seconds and the fight would be over.

Cade could see Bishop's eyes go wide at the realization.

This is for Olsen, you motherfucker, Cade thought, and time stretched as he watched the edge of his sword drive toward Bishop's unprotected neck.

But the Chiang Shih warrior had earned his rank as second in command the hard way, challenging his superiors one by one to mortal combat and he'd yet to lose. He still had a trick or two up his sleeve. As Cade's weapon came slashing toward him, he threw himself the rest of the way to the ground and spun his body around, ignoring the pain in his wounded leg and lashing out with his good one. His heels connected with the backs of

Cade's knees, knocking the Templar commander to the ground beside him.

Cade's sword bounced free of his grip as he hit.

Bishop was on him in an instant.

Bishop pinned Cade's arms and he found himself staring up into his former teammate's face as the other man opened his mouth impossibly wide, revealing the double set of teeth that suddenly seemed to fill his mouth as if out of nowhere.

The teeth descended.

CHAPTER 25

"A SUDDEN REPRIEVE"

WITH HIS ARMS PINNED, CADE knew he had only one chance to save himself and he didn't hesitate to take it. As Bishop's open mouth descended toward his unprotected throat, Cade reared up and slammed his forehead into the other man's as hard as he could.

The blow momentarily stunned Bishop, but that was all the time Cade needed. He wrenched one arm free, then reached down and grabbed his combat knife from the sheath on his calf. With a shout of defiance he shoved the blade through the underside of his enemy's unprotected jaw and deep into his skull.

Bishop stiffened and then toppled over backward.

Letting go of the knife, Cade kicked himself free of Bishop's corpse, climbed to his feet, and staggered a few steps away. His heart was beating wildly and he sucked in a few deep breaths, trying to calm himself in the aftermath of the adrenaline rush.

Behind him, Bishop sat up.

Cade caught the motion out of the corner of his eye and he turned in amazement, just in time to see Bishop reach up, grab the knife by its hilt, and yank it free of his flesh. He tossed it idly to the side.

Around a mouthful of black blood, the other man smiled at Cade.

"The fight's not over yet, Commander," gurgled Bishop.

The Chiang Shih warrior retrieved his sword and climbed slowly to his feet, his fractured knee already healed. Then, as Cade watched in shocked amazement, Bishop's left arm began changing, growing longer and thinner, stretching forward inch by inch, until his entire forearm had become a whip-like appendage with barbed hooks appearing every few inches along its length. Bishop cracked it across the space between them with a vicious snap.

For the first time since the fight started, Cade knew that he was in trouble.

A quick glance showed his sword lying in the dirt between them. Bishop had seen it as well, however, and he advanced, cracking the whip at Cade's head, forcing him back, away from the weapon. Bishop moved forward until he stood over Cade's sword and then used his foot to flip the weapon up and out of the ring, beyond Cade's reach.

But Cade had anticipated such a move and reacted just as swiftly, darting toward the mass of spectators at the circle's edge and grabbing the first weapon he could get his hands on, a long scimitar-like blade that he took right off the belt of an unsuspecting Chiang Shih warrior. There was a general uproar from the crowd at the act, but Cade didn't have time to even glance in that direction for Bishop chose that moment to rush him, hoping to catch him off balance.

Cade backpedaled, parrying Bishop's sword with the flat edge of his own, but then had to practically dive to the side to avoid the lashing strike of the whip that Bishop aimed at his face.

The fight quickly devolved from there.

Bishop took control, forcing Cade to move where he wanted around the ring, the whip lashing out at him time and time again, until Cade's shirt was ripped and his torso bloody.

Maybe he wasn't as sharp as he usually was thanks to the protracted battle he'd engaged in just hours before. Maybe Olsen's loss weighed more heavily on his mind than he realized. Whatever the reason, Cade wasn't at his best

His concentration wavered, just for a second, but that second was enough.

As he ducked to avoid another lashing blow, his foot slipped in the loose sand and he stumbled, off balance.

Bishop made full use of the opportunity. He struck out with the whip, wrapping it around Cade's chest, pinning his sword arm to his side, the barbs cutting cruelly into the bare flesh of his arm and neck.

Cade struggled vainly against the bonds that held him, but it was no use.

He was trapped!

With a quick yank, Bishop pulled him in closer.

"Looks like I'll just have to deliver your corpse instead," Bishop sneered and raised the sword in his other hand, preparing to bring it down for the final strike that would end Cade's life and the combat itself.

Bishop never got the chance.

A sudden whistling sound shot past Cade's ear and in its

wake Bishop reared up in pain, the feathered end of a crossbow bolt sticking out of his left eye socket.

Several other bolts followed in quick succession, striking him about the face and neck.

Bishop toppled over backward for the second time that day, taking Cade with him.

A roar went up from the assembled Chiang Shih as they realized they were under attack. It was answered by a literal rain of crossbow bolts as the Templar knights that had surrounded the camp during Cade's duel with Bishop brought the full might of their numbers to bear against the enemy.

Both sides surged together.

Cade fought to untangle himself from Bishop, all the while expecting some passing Chiang Shih soldier to kill him before he'd managed to do so, but he freed himself and staggered to his feet unharmed. Or at least no worse for wear than when he'd gone down.

Pandemonium reigned.

Combatants were everywhere and no sooner had Cade regained his feet that he was swept up in the maelstrom, forced to defend himself against Chiang Shih warriors hell bent on survival. He fought off two such creatures and turned to take on a third, only realizing it was Riley at the last moment. The other man grinned at him and then eviscerated a nearby opponent with a sudden thrust of his weapon.

They fought until there weren't any more Chiang Shih left to fight. Bodies littered the ground all around, but when it was over the only ones left standing were members of the Order.

Cade found a clear spot and all but collapsed to the ground. He was joined a moment later by Riley, who began using a battlefield med kit to bandage Cade's most grievous wounds.

"You had me worried there for a minute or two," Riley said, as he cleansed one of the lacerations on Cade's shoulder.

"Makes two of us. Never figured Johannson would order our rescue, that's for sure."

Riley shook his head. "He didn't. It was Juarez and his men from Charlie Team. When he heard you'd bucked orders to go back for Duncan, he pulled his men off furlough and got here as quickly as he could."

"They must have moved pretty damned quickly."

"Took them three days. Word is he expected to be avenging our deaths, rather than rescuing our hides. The time differential between this world and our own worked in our favor. Now hold still."

The Knight Commander grimaced, but managed not to flinch too much as Riley wrapped the bandage tight.

To keep his attention off Riley's ministrations, Cade looked at the activity going on around them. Several field medics were moving through the group, caring for other soldiers in the same fashion that Riley was doing for him and across the way Cade could see a collection team gathering the bodies of the dead and preparing them for transportation back to the other side of the Veil. That was a job he didn't envy at all.

A few yards away he could see a fellow knight rummaging through the ruins of a nearby tent. At first Cade thought he was just looking for souvenirs, a practice that, while frowned upon, wasn't actually against the Order's Rule, but the other man was putting too much effort into what he was doing for it to be something so trivial.

Curious now, Cade kept watching. Another moment passed before he recognized that it was Davis, the man who'd been tending to Duncan before the fight broke out.

As Riley rummaged in the kit for another bandage, Cade stood.

Davis' actions became more frantic the longer Cade watched. Convinced he'd seen enough, Cade decided it was time to find out what was going on. He began walking toward the other man.

"Davis?"

When the sergeant didn't answer, Cade tried again. "What's the matter, Davis?"

"I left him right here. I know I did!" When the sergeant turned to face him, Cade was shocked to see tears streaming down the man's face.

An unquiet feeling unfurled itself in Cade's gut.

"Left who right here, Davis?"

But the other man had already tuned him out. He began picking through the pile of corpses, tossing aside each one when it wasn't the man he was looking for. "He was right here! Right here I tell you!"

Cade moved forward and grabbed his arm. When the sergeant tried to shake him off, Cade slapped him once across the face, hard.

It was enough to pull the other man out of his frenzy.

"What are you talking about, Davis? Left who right here?"

"Duncan!"

The bottom fell out of Cade's stomach.

"What?"

"When the fighting broke out he was too weak to join us and we needed all hands to defend ourselves against the mob. I made sure he was well-hidden and gave him his sword just in case. But the fighting swept us away from each other and when I got back he was gone."

"Could he have gotten up on his own?"

"Maybe."

But Cade read the unspoken hesitation in Davis' expression and knew it wasn't likely. Duncan had been badly injured. He wouldn't have left his hiding place unless he'd had no other choice. And that meant he'd been under pressure from the enemy.

By now Riley had joined them and Cade quickly filled him in. The master sergeant wasted no time in organizing a search; after all, Duncan was the entire reason they'd come back. It was possible Duncan had moved to another location, either to avoid discovering or to escape a pursuing enemy. Or maybe he'd received help from a fellow knight and was right now sitting among the wounded in the field hospital that had been set up to treat the injured.

Unfortunately, it didn't take long to determine that wasn't the case. Another team began checking the bodies of the dead still left on the field of battle, but that failed to turn up any sign of him either.

In the process they discovered something else. Bishop's body was gone. It wasn't in the Circle of Judgment where Cade had left it, nor had it been collected with the other by the clean up squad.

Riley was in the midst of giving Cade an update on the situation, when shouts drew their attention. One of Juarez' men was gesturing to them from the edge of camp, waving them over. Cade and Riley lost no time in joining him.

"Look!" the man said, pointing at a spot in the midst of a set of tracks leading away from the camp.

At first Cade didn't see it, but then he bent closer and the glint of gold caught his eye.

It was a Templar signet ring.

It was half buried, as if it had been trampled underfoot.

Or deliberately stepped on to hide it from casual view.

His heart thumping, Cade brushed away the dirt and pulled the ring free of the earth surrounding it. Every member of the Order was given just such a ring on the day they were formally inducted and it was Templar policy to engrave the inside of the band with the man's identification number and date of membership. Chances were good it belonged to either Duncan or Bishop.

He read the number aloud to Riley. As the unit's exec he knew every man's identification number by heart and a moment later Cade had his answer.

It was Duncan's.

But what was it doing here?

Cade considered the situation for a minute, weighing the pros and cons of his next course of action, and then made up his mind. He asked Riley to hold the ring for a moment and then stripped off the glove covering his right hand.

Catching Riley's skeptical look, he explained. "We need to know what happened. The fastest and most accurate way of doing that is with my Gift."

"But you've told me before that using it here in the Beyond can attract unwanted attention."

"True, but right now I don't see any other option. And I think most creatures, supernatural or otherwise, would think twice before attacking a group this size. I've got to take the chance."

Without further discussion, Cade picked up and held the ring in his bare hand.

Weariness.

Pain.

Embarrassment that his comrades have been forced to place

themselves in danger on his behalf.

The sharp poke of a sword blade in the small of his back and a voice in his ear.

"Keep moving. Williams came back for you once, I'm sure he'll do it again."

He stumbled, his injuries and the lack of food taking its toll. But it gave him an idea. As he walked he carefully pulled off his ring and held it in his left hand. A few steps later he stumbled again, only this time he let the momentum take him all the way to the ground, making certain as he did so that the hand with the ring was beneath him. He used the weight of his fall to drive his ring into the ground under him.

When his captor dragged him back up on his feet, he made certain to stumble forward a few more steps, taking the two of them beyond the point where he had left the ring.

With any luck, one of his brothers would find it before things got any worse...

Cade came out of his trance shaking his head, doing what he could to clear away the cobwebs that remained from putting his consciousness in the mind and memories of another.

Riley was looking at him expectantly.

"He's alive. That's the good news. The bad news is that he's not alone. Bishop has him."

CHAPTER 26

"NO ONE GETS LEFT BEHIND"

ROUGHLY TWO HOURS LATER, CAPTAIN Sullivan stepped up to where Cade was making plans with Riley.

"That's it, sir," he said, when he had the other men's attention. "Aside from the two of you, and First Squad itself, the rest of the men have all made the transit back through the gate. Whenever you're ready, we can go."

Cade glanced at Riley, caught his barely perceptible nod in reply, and made his decision. He turned to address Sullivan. "You are going to have to go on without us, Captain. We're staying here."

"I'm sorry?"

It was clear from the captain's expression that he thought he'd heard incorrectly, so Cade spoke slowly and clearly, not wanting there to be any doubt about his intentions.

"Master Sergeant Riley and I are going to remain here for the time being. We still have a man missing and I don't intend to leave until we get him back."

Sullivan took a moment to digest Cade's statement, then visibly steeled himself and said, "Very well, sir, I'll give you whatever assistance I can. Let me just inform the others…"

Cade was already shaking his head. "I appreciate the offer, Captain, but I can't allow that. With Duncan missing, Olsen dead, and Riley here with me, Echo's command unit is effectively paralyzed." He put his hand on the other man's arm and gently began moving him in the direction of the portal, talking all the while. "As head of First Squad, you're next in the chain of command. I need you to assume control of Echo until I return."

If I return, Cade thought, but didn't say aloud. There was no sense giving the captain reason to insist on remaining.

"We shouldn't be gone more than twenty-four hours, if we're lucky. They don't have much of a head start; two hours, maybe three at the most. If things go well, we should be able to catch up to them, rescue Duncan, and return to our side of reality before you know it."

The Captain protested a few moments longer, but Cade could tell that his heart wasn't in it. And who could blame him? No one in their right mind would want to stay here among the unquiet dead if they didn't have to, including Cade. Yet he was staying nonetheless. He had no intention of abandoning Duncan to whatever fate Bishop had in store for him, at least not without a fight. He was also convinced that this was where he might finally gain some answers to the questions that had been haunting him. About the Adversary. About his wife's demise. Even about his own strange gifts.

The answers were here. He just had to have the nerve to go

out and find them.

And that was exactly what he intended to do.

"When you return, you'll probably find the Preceptor waiting to close the gate. They might even destroy the church, just to make sure the gate can't be opened again. I want you to let them do so."

He explained that he and the master sergeant had another means of returning to the real world and that it was a route that the Chiang Shih were not aware of. By closing the gate, they would be satisfying the Preceptor's demands while at the same time denying that route to any of the enemy that still might be able to make use of it. Cade had no idea how the Chiang Shih had managed to open it in the first place, but he was damned if he was going to leave a route to his side of reality open to any of the other denizens of the Beyond.

He moved down the line, shaking hands with all of them, and wishing them Godspeed on their journey. Taking Sullivan's hand last, he said, "Remember, close down that gateway."

The other man assured him he would and then the foursome moved off, intent on reaching the portal before those waiting on the other side got impatient and decided to act without waiting for their return.

Cade didn't blame them; he wouldn't trust the Preceptor either.

Satisfied that he'd done all he could to protect his men, both here and on the other side of the portal, he turned back to Riley and inclined his head in the direction that they thought Bishop and Duncan had taken a few hours before.

Without another word, the two men set off on the trail of their teammate and friend.

The hunt was underway.

They moved at a good pace, aware that they needed to close the lead that Bishop had on them. They had a lot of distance to cover and every minute was crucial.

They hadn't gone far before they discovered another strange aspect of the Beyond. Time itself seemed to be operating on a schedule unique to each of them. When Cade felt as if only a few moments had passed, for Riley it would seemed like it had been hours. Shortly thereafter their positions would be reversed and it would be Cade who felt as if they had been traveling for hours while Riley was refreshed and ready to go. Their watches were no help, either. Cade's digital refused to work while the hands of Riley's analog model simply spun in a continuous circle counterclockwise.

The terrain grew more rugged as they went, the mountains rising higher and the pathways narrower. An hour into their march they came across the first visible evidence that they were on the right track; a piece of tattered cloth had been partially trampled into the mud and when Riley pulled it free of the earth they could see that it was a portion of Duncan's jumpsuit. Cade wished that he dared use his Sight again, for he desperately wanted to know how his subordinate was holding up under the strain of being a captive, but doing so was an unnecessary risk and he restrained himself. It was clear Duncan had intentionally left the scrap behind for them to find, even going so far as to trample it in the dirt to hide it from Bishop's notice as he had done with the ring, and so Cade was forced to rely on that to keep his hopes up.

They camped that night in a small cave along a narrow mountain trail. They didn't have any rations and so mealtime that night was a sorry affair, with just packs of powdered drink mix added to sustain them. Uncertain of what might be roaming out in the darkness, they also chose to go without a fire.

The latter decision turned out to be fortuitous. Cade had just settled down to get some shut eye when Riley called him from the entrance to the cave. When Cade joined him, the big sergeant pointed out across the darkness in the direction they were travelling.

A campfire burned there, its green glow flickering against the sky like a beacon in the night.

"What do you think?" Cade asked.

Riley answered immediately, as if he'd been considering the very question himself for some time. "Two, maybe three hours. No way to catch them in this darkness though. We're going to have to wait until sunrise."

"I agree," said Cade, but he stood and watched that fire for a long time thereafter, as if hoping he might learn something new.

Eventually, he slipped back inside the cave and tried to get some sleep.

* * *

They got an early start the next morning, setting out in the grey half-light that preceded the dawn. The sighting the night before had reinvigorated them and they hoped to gain some time on their quarry by getting underway at that hour.

The mountains continued as far as the eye could see, but the two moved doggedly onward, thinking that those they hunted would be doing the same.

More than once they were forced to break out the climbing ropes they had brought with them, tying themselves together in case one of them slipped on the narrow trails.

It was just after midday when they entered a narrow chasm

that seemed to have been cut from the living rock around them by a giant blade. It was so narrow that at times they were forced to remove their packs and walk sideways, the stone pushing against their chests and backs, but each time they made it through.

As they emerged from the tight channel through which they'd been passing, they found themselves standing on the edge of a cliff, looking down toward the sea. At the base of the cliff loomed a city, but a city the likes of which they had never seen. Great spires of crystal rose high into the sky, but at angles that hurt the eyes, like the freakish and twisted playthings of a giant, playthings that had gone horrible wrong somewhere between inception and culmination. Dark monoliths of squat stone stood around and between them, a sharp contrast not only in their size and shape but in the simple lines of their design. What appeared to be factories of some kind belched dark smoke into the sky, but the smoke seemed to have a life of its own as it twisted and turned under its own design and often against the wind. A wall rose around the city and a road led from the cliff face somewhere below them right up to the massive gate that barred entrance to the place.

It was like something out of a nightmare, a haven for the damned.

Just beyond the city was a sea of wine-dark waves that crashed against the base of the plateau on which it stood, sending spray hundreds of feet into the air. The water extended out in every direction and looking at it, Cade suddenly felt as if they'd come to the very end of the earth.

Exhausted and hungry, the two Templar knights stared down at this unearthly marvel in sheer amazement, both of them wondering the same thing.

Is this where Bishop had been headed?

As if in answer to their question, two figures appeared on the road far below. One strode forward unhindered, while the other constantly stumbled and fell. Each time it happened the individual in the lead would haul on the rope that bound them together until the second individual climbed wearily to his feet.

The newcomers were too far away to see clearly, but Cade didn't have to see them to know who they were. Something deep inside told him what he needed to know.

He turned to Riley with a smile, pointing them out as he did so.

There was no question in his mind that they had done it.

They had caught up with Duncan.

Now all they had to do was rescue him.

CHAPTER 27

"NECROPOLIS"

D UNCAN STARED UP AT THE city walls before him in
numb amazement. Nothing he'd seen so far could
have prepared him for this. Discovering that a place
like the Beyond existed at all had been disconcerting enough, but
to find a city of this size and scale here in the midst of it defied
all logical explanation. It was more than he could take.

He was exhausted, both mentally and physically. His body
was battered and bruised from the beatings he'd taken and his
broken ribs screamed in pain every time his upper body moved.
The fever from the infection in his shoulder wasn't helping
either. Or at least that's what he thought it was, though it was
unlike any infection he'd ever seen. Thick, black pus was leaking
from the center of the wound while the skin surrounding it had
been leeched completely of color. But it was the fact that it
pulsed completely out of sync with his heartbeat that really
unnerved him.

Like it had a heartbeat of its own.

He didn't want to think about the implications that thought brought along with it.

Bishop passed something to the guards at the gate and then pushed his way through the crowd into the city proper, dragging Duncan along with him. His captor had apparently been here before, for he moved swiftly and surely through the crowded city streets, intent on some destination only he knew.

Weary from their forced march and the pain of his injuries, Duncan was reduced to stumbling along behind him. He knew he should be concentrating on where they were going just in case he managed to find a way to free himself, but the streets all looked the same to his fever-addled mind and it was all he could do to keep himself upright. Bishop wouldn't stop if Duncan lost his footing; he knew that from previous experience.

After what seemed like hours of wandering up one street and down another, Bishop entered a large outdoor marketplace and stopped at a stall near the far end. A noxious smell hung over the place and Duncan found it difficult to breathe through the fumes.

The proprietor was a large man in dark clothing and a rubber apron that stretched from his chest to just above his feet. He grunted a welcome at Bishop, giving Duncan the sense that the two of them had done business together before, and then gave a sharp call toward the rear of his shop.

Duncan glanced around, taking in the open furnaces in which green-grey flames burned with cold light, the anvils, and the barrels of iron tools scattered throughout the place. Even to his fever-addled mind it was enough to suggest that he stood in some kind of smithy.

Bishop's next request confirmed it.

"Put him in chains," he said.

It was enough to rouse Duncan from his fog. He glanced wildly around, trying to gauge where the threat was going to come from, but by then it was too late. The blacksmith's assistant, having quietly come up behind the trio, kicked Duncan's legs out from under him and Duncan hit the ground hard enough to knock the wind out of him. As he struggled to suck air into his lungs, the assistant grabbed his arms and yanked them upward so that they lay across a nearby anvil.

The blacksmith worked quickly, grabbing a nearby barrel and dumping a thick grey substance from its depths onto Duncan's wrists. The stuff was icy cold, so cold that his heart skipped a beat, but the blacksmith never hesitated, reaching in with his bare hands and sculpting the substance into the shape he wanted.

Before Duncan even had the chance to object it was over.

The blacksmith released Duncan's hands with a satisfied grunt and they fell back into his lap, far heavier than before. In place of the rope a set of iron manacles now encircled each wrist, with a two foot piece of chain dangling between them. Duncan stared at them, repulsed and fascinated at the same time. The metal was cold and where it touched him it seemed to leech the warmth right from his flesh. Even more distressing where the faces in the surface of the metal, faces he kept seeing out of the corner of his eyes, faces with the lost and tortured expressions of the damned.

But it was the strange keening sound that the metal gave off, as if the dead themselves were bound up in his chains which bothered him the most.

After all he'd been through this last was too much for Duncan.

"Get them off!" he screamed in a high, shrill voice. Somewhere in the back of his mind he knew that wasn't a good sign, but he didn't care. He had to get these things off of him! He pushed frantically at the manacles, first with one hand and then the other, shoving with all his strength, trying to force them over the base of his palms, anything to get them off his skin. The others laughed at his antics, but he didn't stop until the last of his meager strength was spent and his hands were bloody from his efforts.

The chains hadn't budged.

Help me, Lord. Help me.

But only his enemy answered him. "On your feet!" Bishop demanded and punctuated his order with a sharp kick to Duncan's leg.

The Templar knight climbed wearily to his feet, his morale shaken and his strength all but gone. He could only watch dully as Bishop hooked a longer piece of chain to the length that stretched between the manacles on his wrists. A leather handle had been attached to the other end of that chain. Bishop removed a gold ring from one finger, which the blacksmith accepted as payment, and the handle was given to Bishop, who used it like a leash to drag Duncan along behind him as they left the shop.

They only traveled a few blocks before Bishop knocked on the door of another establishment. A gruff voice answered and Bishop replied in the same tongue. Duncan couldn't understand them, but from the tone and the quick responses it was clear that they were haggling over something. Eventually, the door opened and they were ushered inside.

They were being led down a dark hallway, past open rooms where a variety of creatures stared out at them as they passed. Here a man sat by the window, the decapitated head of his lover resting in his arms, the two of them conversing in low tones. There a woman sat cutting the inside of her thigh over and over again. Each time the blade slashed through her flesh it instantly healed again, which only seemed to drive her to new heights of frustration and deeper cuts of the knife. Each room held some different tableau and in his exhausted state, Duncan wasn't certain if he what he was seeing was hallucination or reality.

They came to a rickety wooden staircase that led to the second story and he stumbled up it in Bishop's wake. Their host, a skeletal old woman dressed in a ragged shawl, brought them to the second room on the right and ushered them inside. Aside from the washbin in the corner, the only furniture was a wooden bed in the center of the room.

Duncan barely made it over the threshold before he collapsed on the floor and immediately fell into a restless sleep.

CHAPTER 28

"UNWELCOME GUESTS"

H OW ARE WE GOING TO get in there?" Riley asked, but Cade could only shake his head. He didn't have an answer.

Not yet, at least.

They spent the next hour watching the traffic on the road below them. A good number of travelers came and went during that time and it quickly became obvious that this must not be the only city of its kind in the Beyond. The variety of travelers was staggering, from lone individuals on foot to long wagon-trains full of people and trade goods. More than a few didn't look human.

Watching them come and go gave Cade an idea. He explained his plan to Riley, who agreed it was their best chance at getting inside. The first step was to get down to the plain below without being seen.

A few minutes of searching helped locate a trail leading

downward. It was more a goat path than anything else, just a thin, barely visible track, but it was all they had and it would have to do.

Thankfully it wasn't too steep. Rather than taking the more direct route straight down, it wound its way around the mountain in a series of alternating switchbacks. They followed it at a slow and steady pace. Eventually they reached the bottom without incident.

The city was out of sight around the edge of the mountain itself, but the road was only a few yards away. The two of them took up position behind a large outcropping of rock that allowed them to see the approach to the city without themselves being seen by anyone on the road.

Then they settled down to wait.

It didn't take long. About ten minutes after they'd settled into place they heard movement on the road. Cade snuck a glance around the boulder behind which he was hiding and saw three individuals headed toward them. They wore hooded robes and walked with their heads down, preventing Cade from seeing them clearly, but they were of roughly the right size and didn't appear too imposing.

They would have to do.

As the trio came abreast of them, Cade gave the signal. He and Riley slipped from their hiding place and snuck up behind the newcomers. A brief scuffle ensued, but the newcomers were no match for the Templar soldiers and soon the three of them were lying unconscious on the ground.

The entire confrontation had taken place in silence and when Cade stripped the robe from the lead figure, he discovered why.

The newcomer had no face!

A blank visage confronted him, a smooth plane unbroken by

mouth, nose or eyes. It was as if the Creator had gotten distracted and moved on to His next project before He'd finished with this one. The sight was strangely unnerving to Cade and he found he couldn't look at the other for long without growing uncomfortable.

Thankfully, he wouldn't have to. Turning away from the body, he donned the man's robe while Riley did the same with one of the others. The robes covered their heads and hid their faces from casual view and that was exactly what Cade had wanted.

They dragged the bodies out of sight behind the rocks. Cade would have preferred to leave them bound and gagged, but he didn't have anything with which to do so. Hopefully they would be inside the city before they revived or were discovered by other travelers.

Carefully, they made their way closer to the city gates, trying to keep behind cover and stay as low as possible, not wanting to be seen by any sentries that might be manning the walls. The sun was just setting and the rocks around them cast long shadows, which made their approach that much easier. When they had closed the distance to less than one hundred yards, Cade hunkered down at the base of a shallow gully and called a halt.

"Now what?" Riley whispered.

Cade grinned. "Now we wait for the right Trojan horse to come along."

It didn't take long. As the sun set the guards took longer in performing their duties and soon a crowd had gathered in front of the gate, waiting. One of the groups waiting consisted of several wagons and a small group of people. More than a few were dressed in dark robes, like those the Templars had confiscated. As the group began to pass inside the gates, Cade saw their opportunity.

"Come on!" he whispered to Riley and clambered up out of the ditch.

They strode swiftly out of the darkness and blended with the crowd. They kept their heads down and their hoods pulled low over their faces. The guards had already passed the group's leaders through and were no longer examining individual members, so the Templars were able to slip inside as if they were part of the caravan.

They stayed with the group just until they were out of sight of the gate. As the caravan moved deeper into the city, Cade and Riley slipped down a side street and away from them.

They were inside the city. All they had to do now was find Duncan.

They took a moment to examine their surroundings. Cade was brought up short by the strange array of buildings before him. A seventeenth-century homestead stood between two gleaming towers of glass as dark as obsidian that looked as if they were blown rather than constructed. Further down the street a monolithic office building built in the blocky style favored by government contractors in the nineteen-fifties stood opposite a three story tenement that seemed to be straight out of a Dickens novel. And he'd be damned if that white church tower peeking through from the block beyond didn't look like an exact duplicate of Boston's Old North Church.

An occasional streetlamp pushed back the darkness, their green-blue flames dancing and weaving inside domes of fuzzy glass.

Riley looked around with distaste. "How are we going to find Duncan in this place?"

"I think our best bet is to just keep moving."

Before he could say anything more, shouts erupted from close by. He turned toward the sound, his hand on the hilt of his weapon, and was nearly bowled over when someone dashed out of a nearby alley and slammed into him.

As he disentangled himself from the newcomer, Cade was astonished to see that it was a young girl. She couldn't have been more than six or seven, with long dark hair bound up in pigtails. She wore a grey shift that hung loosely on her frame and it was clear, from the mud and food stains upon its surface, that it hadn't been washed in some time.

She looked up into their surprised faces and must have seen something reassuring, for she immediately moved to put them between herself and the direction from which she had come and said in a frightened voice, "Don't let them get me!"

Before either of them could say anything, her pursuers arrived on the scene.

There were two of them, big, hulking brutes at least seven feet tall, and they looked like they meant business. Both wore stylized metal masks covering the lower half of their faces and rose up to surround their blood red eyes, masks that appeared to be bolted directly into the skin and bone beneath. Above the masks, their bare scalps were crisscrossed with a web of thick red scars.

A network of similar scars ran across their bare chests and heavily muscled arms, giving the impression that they had been repeatedly whipped at some point in the recent past. Long armored skirts covered their lower extremities all the way down to their booted feet. Both were armed with large curved blades that resembled oversized scimitars. Despite their brutish appearance, they had an aura of authority that was hard to dismiss.

If this is what the city was using for law enforcement, Cade would be quite happy to stay on their good side.

At the sight of her pursuers, the girl cowered.

Enforcer #1 barked something in a language neither Cade nor Riley could understand. When he saw that he wasn't being understood, he raised his weapon in a menacing gesture.

A common language wasn't needed to understand that message.

Out of the corner of his eye, Cade saw Riley's hand drift toward the hilt of his weapon in response. "This isn't our fight," Cade said, though he didn't take his eyes off of the enforcers.

But even as he said it, Cade knew that Riley wasn't going to see things that way. He'd never been to the Beyond, didn't understand that sometimes the most vile creatures were often those that hid under innocent guises. He saw only a defenseless girl being harassed by two bullies, rather than the possibility that the girl, despite her innocent appearance, might actually be the greater danger.

Enforcer # 1 had apparently had enough. He strode forward and reached out for the girl with his free hand, ignoring the Templar warriors completely, as if he knew they wouldn't dare defy him.

CHAPTER 29

"UNDER BLACK SAILS"

GET UP! IT'S TIME TO go."

The command was accompanied by a swift kick to his already broken ribs and Duncan did what he could to stifle a groan of pain. The thin smile of triumph that graced his captor's face seconds later let him know he hadn't been entirely successful.

Just wait, you son of a bitch, wait until I get my hands on you... But he knew that right now he wasn't getting his hands on anyone, no matter how badly he wanted to, as they were still bound in the set of manacles that Bishop had slapped on them the night before. He hadn't been imagining things either; the metal still felt cold and greasy to the touch, just as it had last night, and seemed to squirm against his flesh with a life of its own. It made him sick to his stomach if he thought about it, so he did his best to ignore it and think about other things.

Like how the heck to get out of here.

He rolled over, the chains clanking against each other as he climbed to his feet. His legs were unsteady beneath him and he again wondered if his physical condition was simply a result of being here in the Beyond or if Bishop was surreptitiously feeding on him in the dead of night. Either way, it was clear that something was going on. He hadn't felt this weak in years. His sight was fuzzy, his balance shot, and he couldn't seem to keep track of his thoughts for more than a few minutes no matter how hard he tried.

There was a knock on the door of their room. Bishop opened it slightly, looked out, and then said something to whoever was outside. Duncan could make out the quiet murmur of another voice answering him, but he couldn't understand what was said. Bishop must have been satisfied with the response, however, for he hauled on the length of chain attached to Duncan's manacles and the captive had no choice but to follow.

The hallway was empty when they emerged from the room; whoever had been there was gone. They descended to the main floor and passed through several rooms before reaching another staircase. Unlike the first one, this one descended into the depths of the cellar beneath the structure. No sooner had they reached the bottom of that staircase that they entered a series of tunnels carved from the earth itself, marching ahead into the darkness and quickly leaving the light behind.

The tunnels were cold, dark, and narrow. Despite the lack of illumination Bishop moved unerringly through their depths, hauling Duncan along with him, unmindful of the fact that the other man couldn't see. Time and time again Duncan slammed into the walls as Bishop turned into narrow side passages without giving his captive any warning and before long Duncan had lost all sense of direction, the need to keep from smashing his head into an unseen obstacle requiring all of his concentration and preventing him from memorizing the turns they'd taken thus far.

By the time light from somewhere up ahead began to filter back down the tunnel to them, Duncan was too exhausted to do anything but follow his captor.

The light grew brighter and it wasn't long before they emerged from the tunnel and found themselves on a beach of black sand, facing the open sea. Six-foot torches were jammed into the ground in a semi-circle around the cave from which they emerged, their flames burning that strange green-silver color that Duncan had seen back in the camp.

The sight of the ship anchored out in the harbor brought him to a stumbling halt.

It was like something out of the history books, a three-masted sailing vessel with high sides and square stern. Gun ports could be seen running along the side facing the harbor and Duncan found himself wondering about the sorts of beings that might be manning those weapons in a place like this. The ship rode low in the water, though whether from the style of its construction or because it was heavy with cargo, he couldn't tell. It dawned on him that the torches had been set up as a signal for those aboard the vessel and sure enough, a second, smaller light on the water showed them a longboat halfway between the galleon and the beach. It was clearly headed in their direction and upon seeing it, Bishop smiled in satisfaction.

Duncan realized that he was either going to be handed off to the men in the ship or the two of them were going to take a trip somewhere together.

It turned out to be the later.

Bishop dragged him down to the waterline and there they waited for the longboat to reach them. As it drew closer Duncan could see that there were two men working the oars, while a third stood in the prow holding a lantern, lighting the way.

When they reached the beach the oarsmen jumped out and dragged the vessel up into the beach, allowing the other to disembark without setting foot in the water. The leader strode across the sand and greeted Bishop in a language Duncan didn't understand. The other man obviously did though, for he responded in the same tongue.

He was quite large, seven feet at least, Duncan guessed, with the girth to match. He was dressed in clothes that belonged in another century, high-waisted pants and a ruffled shirt, with sailor's boots on his feet and a thick cloak with a hood tied about his neck to complete the image.

Duncan couldn't see his face but when the other turned in his direction he could see eyes of blazing red there in the darkness beneath the hood. The Templar knight was suddenly happy that that was all that he could see.

Bishop and the newcomer conversed for a few minutes, with Bishop growing angrier with each response he received, until at last he was shouting.

The other man refused to budge, however, and Bishop finally had no choice but to give in.

Calling the other man a thief and a whore beneath his breath, Bishop reached inside his shirt and produced a small cloth pouch which he then handed to the newcomer. The other man, if that was indeed what he actually was, slipped it into the pocket of his cloak without opening it and then gestured toward the longboat behind him.

It was clearly an invitation.

With a harsh yank on the chains, which forced Duncan to stumble forward to keep up, Bishop strode down the beach and stepped aboard the boat.

No sooner were they aboard than the crew pushed the boat back out into the surf, jumped aboard, and headed back toward the galleon waiting in deeper waters.

"You've heard of the Flying Dutchman?" Bishop asked, while staring out across the bay.

Duncan nodded, not taking his eyes off the ship that was rapidly looming closer. Having grown up on the coast and having spent considerable time on the water as a child, the legend of that spectral ship forever doomed to sail the world's oceans was one he'd learned of at an early age.

"You're about to board the vessel on which the legend is based. She's known as the Black Rose and if ever there was a ship that was damned, this is it." Bishop turned to face him, a sneer plastered across his face. "You should be honored. You're the first passenger they've had in more than five hundred years. Living passenger, that is."

Apparently the crew understood the joke for they all laughed along with Bishop and the sound made Duncan's skin crawl.

It didn't take them long to cross the bay and reach the galleon. As they came abreast of the ship, a rope was thrown over the side and caught by Red Eyes where he stood in the prow. Without a word to his passengers he turned and hauled himself up to the deck high above. The remaining crew members stared at Bishop and Duncan, making it clear that they were expected to board the ship in the same fashion.

Duncan lifted his hands toward Bishop.

"There's no way I can climb that rope while wearing these things. If you want me to get up there, you're gonna have to unlock them."

Bishop laughed. "You can climb or you can die. Your

choice." Reaching behind him, he grabbed the rope and quickly climbed out of reach.

"Son of a...." Duncan fumed, but there was little that he could do. Knowing the crew would probably toss him overboard if he didn't follow orders, he grabbed the rope, planted one foot against the side of the boat, and started upward.

His injured shoulder screamed at him, but he ignored it as much as he could. He didn't have any choice. He knew the others wouldn't wait forever; at some point they were going to get annoyed and simply cut the rope, letting him drop, chains and all, into the water below. If that happened, he was dead. The weight of the chains would drag him under and he'd drown. He had to reach the top, by whatever means possible, before that happened.

By leaning back against the rope and shifting his hands slowly upward a few inches at a time, he found he could walk himself, one step at a time, up the side of the ship. The weight of the chains pulled at him, threatened to peel him right off the side of the ship, but he gritted his teeth against the pain and shouldered on.

When he reached the top, rough hands grabbed him and pulled him over the rail. He collapsed in exhaustion, the sweat pouring off him and his arms straining from the pain.

The two crew members who'd brought them back from the beach swarmed up the sides of the ship and the longboat itself was hauled up immediately after them.

Captain Red Eyes strode to the middle of the deck and gave a hoarse shout and the crew jumped to obey his command. Deck hands scrambled up the masts, unfurling great black sails that flapped in the breeze that had suddenly sprung up from nowhere as if at the captain's command, and the navigator spun the wheel to take advantage of it.

A strange sound caught Duncan's attention. It was coming from somewhere above him and when he looked up to see what it was, he couldn't help but gasp.

Faces could be seen in the surface of the sails. Faces of men, women, and children, rising to the surface and disappearing again into the depths, faces of the damned screaming in pain and horror and it was their cries that he'd heard.

For the first time since he'd been captured he had the feeling that he was on his own. Not even God seemed to hear him in this hellish place. As he listened to the cries of the damned and watched the ship carve its way through the seas, he wondered if this was it, if the last thing he would ever see would be the faces of the infernal crew around him.

CHAPTER 30

"FOR THE SAKE OF A CHILD"

As the first of the guards reached past Cade for the girl hiding behind him, the Templar warrior made his decision. He didn't know if the girl was simply a girl, or something more, but right now the guardsmen posed a much bigger threat than she did.

Maybe the guard didn't expect resistance. Maybe he was stupid. Maybe he was just used to getting his own way. Whatever the reason, he was completely unprepared for what happened next.

As the brute reached past Cade, intent on getting a good grip on his intended quarry, the Templar knight drew his weapon and, stepping back, brought it slashing down at the man's exposed arm.

There was a moment of resistance and then the guard's severed arm dropped to the pavement with a wet plop.

For a second there was silence.

Then all hell broke loose.

Blood spurted from what was left of the man's arm, drenching Cade's stolen robe in a fountain of gore. A scream burst from the man's mouth at the same time but Cade was already in motion, having expected it. He kicked the man's legs out from under him, reversed his grip on his sword in one fluid motion, and then drove the blade downward through the man's mouth and out the back of his skull, cutting the sound off in mid-cry.

Riley was moving too, his sword moving in a sweeping arc toward the other member of the security detail, ready to end the fight before it really began.

But the other guard reacted quicker than either Riley or Cade anticipated. He blocked Riley's blow with his own weapon, snatching a strange-looking horn from his belt with his other hand as he did so. As Riley spun back toward him for another strike, the man raised the horn to his lips and blew.

The horrifying shriek issued forth from the other end of the horn, a shriek that was abruptly cut off when Riley expertly parried the man's half-hearted attack and then sank his sword into the soft spot beneath the man's face mask, severing his airway.

As the brute collapsed at their feet next to his former partner both men froze, listening intently.

Had they been heard?

For a moment it was quiet, blessedly quiet, and then, from a few blocks away, came the answering cry of another horn. No more than a moment passed before several other horns joined their voices to the first.

The alarm had been given. Cade didn't doubt that the streets would be full of similar guards in mere moments, but he had absolutely no idea about which way to go. For all he knew, the road before him led right to the guardhouse itself.

Despite his hesitancy, or perhaps because of it, the child they'd just acted to save took charge.

"This way!" the girl shouted. "Hurry!"

Neither Cade nor Riley needed to be told twice. They took off at a dead run, following the girl as she weaved a zigzagging route through the darkened city streets, and before long both of the Echo team members were hopelessly lost.

Shouts sounded from off in the distance behind them and they knew the guardsmen's bodies had been found. Pursuit wouldn't be far behind.

The girl moved confidently forward and at last they came to a rundown, boarded-up structure that stood at the end of a narrow alley. Several of the walls appeared to have been blackened by fire and the stink of soot and burnt flesh hung about the place. The girl disappeared around one side of the structure and the two knights followed. They were just in time to see her push through a doorway half-hidden in the shadows of the nearby buildings.

They stood there a moment, debating, and when they didn't immediately follow she stuck her head back out the doorway. "Hurry!" she cried.

The two men really had no choice but to comply.

They found themselves inside what had once been a restaurant or tavern, some kind of eating establishment. A long bar made of some kind of dark wood, oak or mahogany maybe, stretched down the length of the room and several dusty chairs stood at intervals in front of it. A number of tables and several chairs were scattered throughout the rest of the room, all appearing to have been made entirely from wood, but from the thick layer of dirt and dust that covered them it was immediately obvious that they hadn't been used for some time. The smell of ash was stronger here though there was no sign of the fire that had consumed part of the exterior.

The girl closed the door behind them, held a finger to her lips, and then backed away from the entrance, never once taking her eyes off the door.

Riley and Cade followed suit.

Outside, from the streets, came the sounds of pursuit; men yelling, the tramp of booted feet, even the howl of strange beasts that had apparently been brought in to track them.

Quietly, the Templars drew their weapons, getting ready to defend themselves should their hiding place be discovered.

For a moment, when the creatures outside suddenly began howling in unison, Cade was afraid they'd been found. He braced himself, ready to take down the first intruder through the door, but then the baying receded into the distance and he breathed a sigh of relief.

"I think they're gone," Riley whispered and Cade agreed.

The girl giggled behind them.

Cade spun around and nearly crashed into a short, stocky fellow who had crept up behind them when their attention was on the pursuers outside. Shocked at the man's sudden appearance, Cade went instantly on guard, the tip of his sword only inches from the man's throat.

"Whoa, now! Take it easy there, friend. I didn't mean to creep up on you." He held up his hands in a warding off gesture and smiled to show he meant no harm.

"Who are you? What did you do with the girl?" Cade asked.

The newcomer laughed. "The girl? You mean my daughter, Penelope?"

At the sound of her name the girl poked her head out from

behind the man's thick frame, a shy smile on her face.

"Why, she's right here. And as for who I am, my name's Malevarius and you're standing in my home."

Cade relaxed a little, pulling his sword away from the man's throat but not putting it down completely.

"They helped me escape from the Dreadnoughts, Father. They killed two of them, right before my eyes."

"Two of them now, did they?" For a moment the man's genial expression changed to one of sharp interest, but then the mask was back and the smile flashed a second time.

Introductions were made and once it was established that neither side meant the other any harm, the two Templar knights were invited to stay for the evening meal. Knowing they couldn't return to the city streets while the patrols were still searching for them, Cade saw no harm in agreeing.

Dinner was a mixture of familiar and unfamiliar foods, from the sliced apples that Penelope produced from some hidden pocket inside her shift to the bowl of grayish gruel that Malevarius served them with more than a hint of pride. Cade decided against asking what was in it; the way it seemed to shift and churn of its own accord made him less than anxious to know.

An hour later, their meal finished, Cade took the opportunity to question their host.

"What is this place?"

Malevarius looked around fondly at the ruins of the tavern in which they sat and it was clear that he loved the old place almost as much as he loved his daughter. "Once, it was the finest tavern in all New England. The Black Rose. People came from throughout the Colonies to drink our ale and catch a taste of my wife's mutton pie."

Cade looked around, trying to reconcile the man's description with the ruins in which they sat. "What happened? How'd you end up here?"

"I don't know. There was a fire; I know that. I remember the heat and the flames. I remember escaping into the cold night air with my wife at my side, only to realize that our daughter was still trapped inside. I went back for her." The barman shrugged. "There was the crack of timbers and the next thing I know Penelope and I are here, in this place, with what was left of the Rose still smoldering around us."

For a moment Malevarius' eyes took on a far-off expression and Cade knew he was remembering other times, other places. But then the barman shook himself out of it.

"And the city? Did all of its buildings arrive in a similar fashion?"

Malevarius grinned. "So you noticed the rather eclectic nature of our fine city?" He turned serious. "The City of Bones it's called, though personally I think the City of Lost Souls would be a more appropriate moniker. As far as I know it's always been here and probably always will. It changes from time to time, buildings appearing and disappearing overnight, but the city itself remains the same, a haven for the lost and the damned, perched here at the edge of the Sea of Shades."

Cade wondered just how much he could ask this man.

Sensing his hesitation, Malevarius said, "Come now. You saved my daughter. I'm in your debt. How can I help you?"

Cade and Riley exchanged glances. *Did they dare trust this man?* They needed someone who knew the city, someone who could guide them to the most likely places hiding places, someone who understood the ins and outs of life here in the city. *What other choice did they have?*

"We're searching for a friend of ours who was brought here last night against his will. He's in the company of another man who is holding him prisoner." Cade described them both, and then said, "We lost their trail shortly after entering the city and it's vital that we track them down quickly."

Malevarius listened intently and when Cade was finished the barman called his daughter to his side. He wrote something on a small scrap of paper and then handed it to her. "Take this to Jessup. Ask him to put the word out for information about either of these men. Tell him I'm willing to pay for anything worthwhile."

The girl took the paper from her father's hand, winked at Cade, and disappeared out the back door of the tavern.

Riley rose halfway out of his chair, the concern evident on his face. "Is she going to be all right? What if she runs into one of those patrols?"

Malevarius waved him back into his seat. "It will take more than a couple of Dreadnoughts to capture my girl." Turning to Cade, he said, "There's an informal network in the city. We try to help each other out when we can. If anyone has seen your friend, we'll know in a couple of hours."

They were quiet for a few moments, each lost in their own thoughts, until Cade broke the silence.

"What can you tell me about the Isle of Sorrows or the Lady in the Tower?"

Malevarius stared at him for a moment, surprised, and then looked away. For the first time since they'd come here, he turned evasive. "Nothing. Never heard of them," he said, but it was obvious from his body language that he wasn't telling the truth.

Cade reached out and touched Malevarius, getting him to look up. "It is important. More than you can imagine."

The two men stared at each other. It became a battle of wills, waiting to see who would look away, who would break the link first.

Eventually Malevarius sighed and gave in. "It's an island. A few days travel north of us, across the Sea of Lamentations." He paused, collecting his thoughts. "Years ago, the Isle was a thriving place, a sister city to this one. Trade between us was brisk and it was because of that trade that the lower harbor was built, to allow for more vessels to dock here at one time.

"Word reached us that a new power walked the Isle, a power stronger than any that had been seen before, a power known only as the Dark One. He laid claim to the city, to the isle itself even, and when the city fathers resisted he proceeded to destroy them, seemingly without effort. Enraged by their resistance, the Dark One set out to raze the entire city."

Malevarius scowled. "They never stood a chance. Fire broke out, a strange witchfire that consumed stone and steel alike. It swept through the city in moments, destroying everything it touched. A few refugees reached us later, those who had already been aboard their ships when the fighting broke out and were able to put to sea before the conflagration that consumed the city could reach them. The sea was renamed in the wake of the tragedy, becoming the Sea of Lamentations, so named for all the grief that had been shed upon its waters."

His expression turned wistful. "The rumors started shortly after that, rumors about the Lady who'd stood against the Dark One, who'd fought alone against their foe to give the others the time they needed to get away. They say that though the Dark One was able to defeat her, her power was so great that he was unable to destroy her completely. He was forced to imprison her instead, in a tower that rose over the city, a tower built overnight by the hands of a thousand demons summoned just for that task."

"The Lady in the Tower," Cade said, wonderingly.

Malevarius nodded. "Some say they've seen her. Here, in this city, free of her chains and the confines of the Tower. They say that at the moment when all is lost, when death looms near and there is no way out, she sometimes appears to those who believe and rescues them from certain destruction, just as she rescued those in the city before its fall."

"And you? Do you believe that?" Cade asked.

Malevarius shrugged again, "I don't know what I believe. I've never seen the Lady myself, but I suppose anything is possible, especially in this god-forsaken place. I can tell you that I've seen the Tower, once, when the ship I was on drifted off course and came too close to the Isle. It rises above the ruins, a long narrow arm thrust up into the sky, and something about it gives one a deep sense of loneliness and despair just to look at it."

After that, Malevarius didn't want to talk much and the conversation petered off. Perhaps it was for the best, because the Templars were exhausted and they needed to get some rest. If word came that Duncan had been found, they were going to have to move quickly. The barman fetched them some blankets and, believing themselves to be secure, the two men settled down for some much needed sleep.

CHAPTER 31

"DON'T PAY THE FERRYMAN"

C ADE AWOKE TO FIND RILEY kneeling beside him, gently shaking his arm. Malevarius stood just behind him, a nervous scowl on his face. Of his daughter Penelope, there was no sign.

As Cade rubbed the sleep from his eyes and gathered together his gear, his partner filled him in.

"One of Malevarius' contacts has sent word that Duncan was seen less than an hour ago, headed for a ship anchored just offshore. And get this - rumor has it that the vessel is bound for the Isle of Sorrows."

A flare of hope surged in his chest. "Can we catch them?" Cade asked, looking toward Malevarius.

Malevarius shrugged. "I think I can get you passage on another ship. A captain I know owes me a favor."

Cade nodded at the innkeeper. "Thank you."

The other scowled. "Don't thank me. You're the one foolish

enough to make the journey."

Cade and Riley still had the hooded robes they'd stolen before entering the city. The dark color of the fabric hid the bloodstains reasonably well and they used them again to hide their features from casual view.

Once they were ready, the innkeeper led them out into the predawn darkness. The sun was just edging its way over the horizon and a thick fog still hung about the city, but Malevarius was taking no chances. He avoided all of the major thoroughfares, sticking instead to the back streets and alleys where traffic would be minimized and there would be less chance of encountering a patrol.

Eventually, they came upon a thick wall that stretched along the far side of the street. Malevarius motioned them in close.

"This is the outer wall of the city. We have to follow it to the Winding Stair and from there make our way down to the wharves below."

"Roger that," Cade said and gestured that they should continue on.

Eventually the wall itself came to an end and the trio cautiously peered around it at the scene splayed out below.

A massive stairway, at least several hundred feet in length and wide enough to allow ten men to walk abreast, led down from where they stood to the shoreline below. An equally ambitious series of docks had been constructed there in the shelter of the bay. A number of ships were currently docked along the wharves, vessels from a bewildering array of times and cultures. A Viking longship, or drakkar, was moored near a modern sailing yacht, like those used in the America's Cup race. A World War II freighter was just entering the bay, its funnels pouring out a thick column of black smoke, while by its side sailed a galleon that would have looked perfectly at home in the waters off the coast of the New World in the days of the Colonies. Like the mishmash of architectural styles that made up the city itself, the vessels in the harbor were cast offs from several historical periods, a hodgepodge of style and purpose.

They descended the stair and entered the wharf district, eventually reaching the docks themselves. Malevarius was careful to approach only those captains that he knew personally, doing what he could to limit their exposure.

Two hours and eleven ships later, they were forced to admit defeat. None of the captains were willing to take them on as passengers, particularly when the captains discovered where they wanted to go. Malevarius pleaded with several of them on the Templars' behalf, but the answer was always the same.

Not a chance.

The three of them knew that time was running out. So far they had avoided any sign of the authorities, but word was bound to leak out about the two strangers looking for passage to the Isle of Sorrows and that was enough to gain them official attention, never mind their culpability in the death of the two Dreadnoughts the night before. And every passing moment allowed Bishop to put more distance between them, taking Duncan farther and farther out of their reach.

Cade was all but ready to steal a ship and strike out on their own, when he noticed a tall hooded figure staring at them from the shadows of a nearby doorway, a long, narrow shaft in one hand. Something about the figure was familiar.

Malevarius noticed the other's interest at about the same time and he took Cade's arm, turning him away from the stranger. "You don't want anything to do with them."

Curious, Cade resisted. "Why not? What's wrong?"

"That's one of the Ferrymen. No one sane has anything to do with them."

"The Ferrymen?" Something stirred at the back of Cade's mind and then the memory came flooding back, he and Duncan trapped in an unfamiliar part of the Beyond during the operation against the Necromancer, deep water at their backs and spectres closing in on them from the front, the strange hooded figure piloting the narrow reed boat that had pulled them off the shoreline just in time, a figure that had turned out to be Gabrielle in disguise.

He broke the barman's hold on his arm and rushed toward the hooded figure, shouting, "Gabrielle!"

He skidded to a stop directly before the other, hope flaring in his chest, and only then realized his mistake.

This was not Gabrielle.

The Ferryman was at least seven feet tall and he seemed to tower over Cade. His robes hid him from view, but the hand holding his staff was withered, the skin stretched so tightly over the bones that it looked as if they might burst through the flesh at any second.

"Sorry. My mistake," Cade said and began to back away.

The Ferryman's hand shot out and grabbed Cade's arm.

A voice sounded in his head.

"You are looking for passage? I will take you."

Cade was standing there, staring in dumb amazement, when his companions reached him.

"We're very sorry, good sir. Completely our mistake," said Malevarius, "if you would just let go of my friend we will be moving on and won't be any further burden."

As if from a distance Cade heard himself say, "It's okay. We're going with him."

The Ferryman released him and stepped back, waiting.

"What!" Malevarius said. He pulled Cade and Riley off to the side, speaking in an urgent whisper so as not to offend the Ferryman.

"No one travels with the Ferrymen, if they can help it, no one. Heaven only knows what they want or what happens to those who accept travel, for none have ever been seen again."

But Cade wasn't to be deterred. Something about the connection between Gabrielle's appearance as one of their number and the way the Ferryman had sought him out felt right to him. He knew, *knew*, that they were supposed to make the journey in this fashion, though he couldn't have told his companions just how.

Cade asked Malevarius to handle the negotiations, insisting when the other man objected, and at last he agreed to do so. As the barman walked over to the Ferryman, Cade turned to Riley.

"This is our way to the Isle. I'm sure of it."

"Fine with me, boss. Just so we get out of this city before any more of the Dreadnoughts show up, I'll be happy."

And so it was settled. Malevarius returned, telling them their passage had been arranged, and the three men said their goodbyes. The Templars then followed the Ferrymen a few hundred yards farther down the docks to where his boat waited for them.

Seeing it, Cade almost changed his mind.

It could just barely be called a boat. It was about fifteen feet long, a narrow vessel made from some kind of reed-like substance, without sail or even obvious means of locomotion. There wasn't much room and it was a good thing that the knights didn't have much equipment with them; it probably wouldn't have fit on board. A narrow bench on either side of the prow was the only place for passengers to sit, unless they chose the floor.

The Ferryman indicated they should board the vessel with one sweep of his arm and, before he could think twice and change his mind, Cade clambered aboard.

Riley quickly followed.

CHAPTER 32

"THE SEA OF LAMENTATIONS"

SCHEWING THE SEATS, WHICH DIDN'T look large enough to hold them, the two knights settled down on the floor of the boat, doing what they could to get comfortable despite the narrow confines. Once they were ready, the Ferryman stepped to his place at the rear of the boat and placed his staff over the side.

Cade expected him to use the staff the way you would use a pole on a raft, pushing it against the river bottom and moving them one stroke at a time, but the Ferryman apparently didn't need to. No sooner had the staff entered the water that the boat got underway, as if by magick. They glided away from the dock, smoothly navigated around the numerous boats moving in and out of the harbor and in no time at all were in deeper water, headed for the open sea.

The passage to the Isle took several hours. Cade tried a number of times to engage their captain in conversation, but each time the Ferryman simply looked at him, not saying a word, and eventually Cade gave up. Riley, too, seemed reticent to talk and so Cade spent most of the journey lost in thought, wondering what was left in store for him when he returned to the other side.

"Land ho!" Riley shouted, sometime later, and Cade looked up to see a vast island rising out of the water in the distance. As they drew closer, they began to make out details.

It was big, probably several miles in length, at least from this angle. It was covered in a deep green carpet of jungle and the cone of its volcano rose high over the rest of the island. Cade glanced upward, searching for any sign that the mountain was still active, and froze at what he saw.

There, high above the jungle, was a massive hole in the sky. That was the only way he could describe it. It was as if two great hands had grasped the fabric of the sky and torn it asunder, opening up a giant rift in the fabric of reality.

"He will find me across the Sea of Lamentation, on the Isle of Sorrows beneath the tear in the sky."

Cade's heart beat faster. They had followed Duncan to the one place in the world Cade wanted to venture to most. Now all he had to do was rescue both his friend and the soul of his wife.

With Riley at his side, he felt like he could do anything and he clapped his companion on the shoulder, both of them laughing aloud at having reached their destination.

The Ferryman gasped, the first sound either of his passengers had heard him make, and they twisted around to see what he was looking at.

Off to starboard a huge wave was rushing toward them. It had to be at least twenty feet tall and on its heels came a wall of darkness so thick that it had to be unnatural.

In seconds the storm was upon them.

It raged like a living thing, the winds howling around them, the waves cresting high overhead and then smashing down with the force of an artillery barrage, threatening to throw them overboard into the hungry maw of the sea itself. The Templars clung to the gunwale, their legs braced against the sides of the narrow boat, terrified that at any moment the boat would be overturned.

The Ferryman stood in defiance against it all, never leaving his post, keeping one end of his staff in the water at all times, keeping them upright and afloat against the power of the maelstrom seemingly with his will alone.

They were at the mercy of the sea and wind, however, and it quickly became obvious that they were being forced far off course, the island receding so quickly in the distance and the boat being tossed about so much by the storm that they lost all sense of direction. And still, the storm beat at them, driving them farther and farther off, tossing and turning them amongst the waves. When it got particularly bad, he roped himself against the side of the boat, tossing the other end to the two knights and pantomiming that they should do the same.

Riley and Cade were only too happy to comply.

Eventually, the power of the storm lessened and then finally petered out.

Seated in several inches of water, soaked to the skin and exhausted from the ordeal, the two men breathed a sigh of relief when the Ferryman untied himself from the rope and looked out at the water around them.

The sea was calm, quiet even.

But in the silence after the storm, a new problem reared its head.

The Ferryman stood in the prow of the boat, staff in hand,

looking out toward the horizon. After a moment he moved aft and repeated the process, gazing off into the distance so intently that, watching him, Cade could almost imagine that he was searching for the very secrets of life itself rather than the direction in which to resume their travel.

This went on for several moments, back and forth, until Cade began to grow concerned. He was just about to say something when the Ferryman seemed to make up his mind and took up his customary position near the rear of the boat. He lifted his staff, preparing to get them underway, only to put it back down again without ever placing it in the water.

Cade's concern grew into alarm.

"What's wrong?"

The Ferryman turned its hooded countenance toward him but didn't say anything.

"We're lost, aren't we?" Cade asked.

Cade didn't expect an answer. The Ferryman had yet to say anything, even in the midst of the danger they'd faced, and the Templar knight had become convinced that their hooded guide was incapable of speech. So when the Ferryman looked out across the dark waters surrounding them and said, "Yes," in a croaking rasp that sounded as if his voice hadn't been used in years, perhaps decades, Cade was understandably surprised.

Apparently Riley was too.

"Lord help us," Echo's executive officer said.

For once, Cade agreed with him.

Then Cade noticed Riley was staring at him oddly.

"What is it?" he asked.

Riley, completely at a loss for words, could only point.

Cade looked down, wondering just what had his teammate spooked so badly.

The feather he wore about his neck was straining against the leather thong to which it had been attached, lifting itself up off his skin and pointing away across the open water.

A voice echoed in Cade's mind, the voice of the angel who had given him the strange trophy.

"You will need this, son of Adam."

Now, at last, Cade understood why.

Apparently the Ferryman did as well, for no sooner had he seen the direction in which the feather was pointing than he put his staff in the water, turned the boat in that direction, and gotten them underway.

Cade had always believed that the feather had belonged to the angel Baraquel, the enemy vanquished by the Echo Team in the depths of the Eden Complex several months before. After all, it had been given to him shortly after Echo had stood down from that mission. Now he suspected that he'd been wrong, that the feather actually originated from the wings of Cade's nemesis, the Adversary, and right now it was leading them to him in much the same way a compass needle with point toward magnetic north. Somehow the feather and the Adversary were connected.

Their journey continued. When it began to get dark, the Ferryman took a brass lantern out of a storage chest and hung it on hook attached to his staff, apparently just for that purpose. He passed a hand over one of its grimy windows and a deep blue flame sprung up inside, lighting their way. A few hours later Riley spotted land on the horizon for the second time that day.

It didn't take them long to get close enough to see that they had once more reached their destination. There was the same spit of land jutting out into the ocean, the same mountain rising high above the shoreline. And the most telling feature of all, that same strange tear in the sky high above the jungle that covered most of the island.

They were still several hundred yards from shore when the boat began to slow. Cade turned to ask what was happening, only to be handed a large pole with an iron hook on one end. Riley received one just like it. Without a word the Ferryman turned back to his station. When Cade stood there, not understanding the Ferryman waved him toward the front of the boat.

Cade moved to the prow and looked down. Now he understood. Thick, twisted strands of dark colored seaweed were bunched together ahead of them, forming a carpet-like structure that stretched ahead of them almost all the way to the beach. Clearly the boat was not going any farther unless they created a path through the obstruction, which was what the hooks were for.

He dipped his pole into the water and tried to push the weeds aside. They parted slightly, but didn't move. Cade pushed the pole deeper.

It struck something solid.

Frowning, he did it again, watching as the weeds seemed to bob for a moment in the water and then settled back down again as the pressure at the end of the staff was released. Cade turned the hook, felt around until it seemed to lodge against something solid, and then pulled.

A hideously waterlogged corpse bobbed to the surface of the water, its features twisted into a parody of a smile.

Cade stumbled backward, bile filling his throat.

The weeds were not weeds at all, but the tangled hair of a thousand corpses, each one standing upright in the shallow water leading to the beach.

To get to the shore, they were going to have to pull them

aside one at a time, creating a route for the Ferryman to use in getting them close enough to disembark.

The two Templars set about their task.

It was exhausting work. The corpses had been in the water for some time, growing heavy as water accumulated in their tissues, but had also been preserved in some strange way to keep them from decaying. It took both men to move a single corpse and often another would bob directly into the path to replace the one they had just removed. Both men were forced to turn away more than once, the expressions on the bodies of the dead oddly unsettling to the battle-hardened warriors. It was almost as if some sorcery had been placed on the bodies for just that purpose.

They made slow progress, but progress it was, and some time later they finally managed to break through the corpse field and enter cleaner water on the other side.

They were close enough now to see the slash in the sand where another boat had been temporarily beached and to make out the double set of footprints that ran up the beach to the jungle beyond.

Even more encouragingly, there weren't any tracks leading back down the beach from the treeline.

Whoever had landed was apparently still on the island.

CHAPTER 33

"THE ISLE OF SORROWS"

THE FERRYMAN BROUGHT HIS VESSEL up as close to the beach as possible. Riley and Cade jumped out and waded through the knee-deep water until they reached the shore. When they turned back to thank their mysterious benefactor, they discovered that he had already turned his vessel around and was headed for deeper water.

"Great. Just try finding a taxi out here," Riley said and despite the position they were in, Cade couldn't help but laugh.

The tracks they'd seen from offshore were easy enough to locate with just a few minutes of searching. Drawing their weapons, they followed them up the beach and into the trees beyond.

They hadn't gone more than a few hundred yards when they found Bishop.

Or, rather, what was left of him.

His severed head had been impaled on one end of a sharpened

stake. The other end had been driven into the ground in the middle of the trail, eliminating any chance that they could have passed this way without seeing it. The ripped and shredded remains of the rest of his body lay scattered in and out of the trees just beyond, many of them impossible to identify.

The two Templar warriors stopped and carefully surveyed the area around them, wary of an attack, but the woods around them seemed empty. Whoever had done this appeared to have moved on.

Then Bishop's head spoke to them.

"Aren't you even curious, Officer Cade? About why I'm in your house? Why shot your partner and am holding your wife hostage. Aren't you even curious about why I'm going to kill you both?"

The voice chilled Cade down to his very core, for it was a voice out of his past, a voice he never expected to hear again, a voice from that horrible summer day when a thing posing as a human killer had invaded his home and slaughtered his beloved wife right before his eyes.

It was the voice of the Adversary.

Riley had been friends with Cade long enough to know the personal relevance behind those particular phrases and he shot a quick glance at his commander.

"Stay cool. He's trying to rile you," Riley said, sotto voce.

Fighting to restrain the rage coursing through him, Cade could only nod, not trusting himself to speak. He knew Riley was right; the Adversary was baiting him, trying to goad him into acting rashly, just as he did in his recurring dream. Cade also knew that if he gave into that anger, if he let it control him and guide his decisions, the battle would be over before it even began.

After a moment, when it was clear that their enemy was not waiting for them amidst the shadows of the trees and when Cade had managed to reign in his anger to a manageable level, they skirted around the gruesome trophy in the middle of the trail and continued onward. The trail led deeper into the woods and they followed it until a clearing opened up before them.

As Cade emerged from the trees, he stopped in amazement. There before him was the town from his dreams, from the blackened buildings lying in crumbling heaps on either side of the road to the occasional strange-looking plant that had managed to force its way up through the concrete surface into the dim light and warm air above. The sky had grown dark, slate-grey storm clouds laced with silver and green lightning having rolled in from the horizon and were now casting their shadows over the town below. The air was heavy with impending rain and the electrical tension of the growing storm. Even the wind had made its scheduled appearance, just as it had in his dream, its voice like those of a thousand lost souls forever begging for deliverance at exactly the same moment.

"Where the hell are we?" Riley whispered, the fear evident in his voice for perhaps the first time since they'd entered the Beyond. He watched the shadows around them stretch and move as if under their own accord. Cade didn't have the heart to tell him that he thought he'd gotten it right the first time; that they were, indeed, in Hell itself.

They stood at the edge of the City of Despair.

But while the landscape before him resembled his dream in many ways, there were differences, too. On the far side of the town, where the landscape had simply faded into nothingness in his dreams, there now stood a massive white tower that stretched skyward, reaching for the clouds above. Hovering over it was that awesome tear in the sky, that rip in the fabric of reality, that they had been following ever since they first laid eyes upon it, like the star that led the three wise men to Bethlehem. He didn't know what that thing was, wasn't even sure he wanted to know, but seeing it gave him hope. The fact that things were not identical to his dreams meant that the future was not preordained, that the events coming toward them were not written in stone, that the way they played out in reality did not have to mirror the way they had ended in his dreams.

No sooner had he come to that conclusion that a lance of pain shot through his hand, flashing up his arm and across the damaged side of his face, just as it always had in his dreams.

Which meant any minute now the Adversary should be making his appearance...

As if on cue, the sound of booted feet striking pavement echoed back to him from the other end of the road and a dark figure stepped out to bar their way.

The Adversary had arrived.

All the years of pent up hatred exploded through Cade in that instant. Every stolen moment, every potential memory, every lost laugh and cry and shout of joy, all the things he was never able to share with his wife because of the actions of the thing standing before him, all of it came roaring together inside his heart and mind, screaming in anguish at what had never been.

Cade gave into that flood, let it bend him, break him, never once considering that losing control might be the very thing that the Adversary had planned.

Dimly, in the back of his mind, he could hear Riley shouting, "No, Cade! No!" but it was way too late.

With a scream of rage and loss, Cade charged the Adversary.

Just as he always had in his dreams.

Laughter rang out, echoing across the ruined landscape, and the Adversary suddenly straightened to its true height, throwing off its concealing robes to stand revealed in all its majesty and power.

The fallen angel stood at least eight feet tall, clothed in gleaming armor and brandishing a sword that shone like the sun. It hurt just to look at him and Cade was forced to hold up a hand to shield his face from the glare even as he continued his precipitous charge forward.

Foolish acts often have unwelcome consequences and this was no exception to the rule. Even as Cade rushed forward the Adversary raised his free hand and pointed it at Cade. A brilliant flare of red-black power shot forth, striking Cade in the chest and throwing him violently to the ground. Before he could get up the Adversary struck out again, and again, hammering him with each successive strike, pounding him into submission. Arcane energy flashed through Cade, short-circuiting his nervous system, sending his limbs flapping and his teeth clenching and unclenching uncontrollably. His body flopped about the ground like a fish out of water and pain flooded over and through him, growing stronger and stronger with each successive strike from the Adversary's hands.

Cade could hear himself screaming, could hear the Adversary echoing his cries with crazed laughter, and then it all became too much. The last thing he remembered was the thunder booming overhead and the lightning flashing and crackling around him.

The storm's arrived, he thought, and then the darkness took him.

CHAPTER 34

"THE ADVERSARY, AT LAST"

W HEN CADE REGAINED CONSCIOUSNESS SOME
unknown amount of time later, he found himself
spread-eagled against a nearby wall, his arms and
legs stretched out to either side by an unseen force that held him
in place as surely as if he had been embedded in the concrete
itself. No matter how hard he struggled, he couldn't so much as
turn his head, never mind free one of his limbs. It was hopeless;
he was completely at his captor's mercy.

He was much deeper in the city, apparently, for he could just
barely glimpse what he thought was the base of the white tower
out of the corner of one eye.

He wondered if Gabrielle was up there somewhere, high
above. If she could see him, if she knew he had come for her.

Some rescue this was turning out to be.

The sound of someone approaching drew his attention. A
man stepped out in front of him. His skin was dark, his hair

equally so, and he was dressed like anyone you might pass on the street of an average neighborhood.

The newcomer smiled and in that smile was every cross word ever spoken, every insult ever made, every act, no matter how small or large, that had harmed another human being, and Cade knew that he was looking at the Adversary in another of his many guises.

Just to be certain, Cade triggered his Sight, figuring he no longer had anything to lose by using his gifts.

His mystical vision helped peel back the layers of deception, revealing the true face of the creature standing before him, and what he saw made him jerk back in horror.

His attention was drawn first to the great wings rising over each shoulder, their once tar black feathers long since tattered and torn, stained with the ash of the great city around them, identical to the one Cade wore around his neck. Where the feathers had fallen away completely a thick pink membrane could be seen stretching beneath, its surface covered with a fine web of crimson veins that pulsed with what seemed to be life of their own.

The flawless beauty of its face had been replaced by a seeping ruin, a canvas of open sores that oozed a dank smelling fluid which in turn were interspersed with layers of flesh that hung loosely from the bone, visual evidence of the corruption that lay within its soul. One eye festered with rampant infection and seeing it, Cade finally understood that both he and Simon Logan, the Necromancer, had been marked as one of the Adversary's own.

The very idea made him want to vomit.

Asharael raised a hand and Cade's gaze was drawn involuntarily to its overlong fingers. They had to be six inches or more in length, topped by curving yellow nails that had been sharpened to a point. Cade followed their length to where they pointed out toward the horizon.

"Look!" Asharael whispered and in his voice Cade could hear every lover's seductive promise, every con man's intrepid game. Out there in the darkness endless vistas opened up before him even as he watched, each one a vision of paradise, worlds where he was the ultimate authority, where he waded in wealth and riches, where beautiful women waited at his beck and call to fulfill his every whim, regardless of how base or how refined his demands.

"This could all be yours. Power beyond your imagination. Wine, women, and riches to do with whatever you will."

Cade said nothing, waiting for what it would cost, knowing that every agreement, especially one with the Enemy, had a price. He did, however, drop his Sight, both unable and unwilling to look at the Adversary's true form another moment longer.

The Adversary suddenly stepped closer and grasped Cade's chin. Seemingly without effort he pushed Cade's chin upward, so that Cade could see the churning hole in the sky above. It seemed larger now, more ominous even than it had before, and Cade didn't know if that was because he was closer to it or if it had fundamentally changed in the time since he'd set foot on the island.

"You're looking at the Barrier, the veil of power between this world and the next," said the Adversary. "You have the power to control the doorway between the two."

Cade's head was pulled back down, until he was looking at the Adversary once more. The other released him and stepped back, smiling.

"All you have to do is open that doorway and I will let you and your friends go free."

Cade refused to reply. *Go to hell, you bastard*, he thought.

The smile never left the Adversary's face. "Not enough for your tastes? Perhaps you're expecting me to sweeten the pot? Well let's see, what might entice you to do as I ask…"

Mockingly, the Adversary snapped his fingers. "I know. Your precious wife."

Without waiting to see Cade's reaction, the Adversary turned away toward the white tower and pointed. Cade felt a rumble beneath his feet and white blocks of masonry began falling from somewhere up above, crashing down around him with thunderous impact.

Cade's head was suddenly free and he was able to turn and look at the white tower.

Aside from a small ring of stones making up the rear wall, the entire tower was gone. The Adversary had torn it down without laying a single finger on it. But that wasn't what caught Cade's attention.

In the middle of the lowest floor of the tower was a sumptuous bier of gold and platinum.

On that platform lay Cade's dead wife, Gabrielle.

Cade was unable to speak.

He knew it wasn't physically his wife; her body was still back in the real world, as far as he knew, guarded by Elizabeth Clearwater and her hedge magick. But Elizabeth had said that Gabrielle's essence, her soul if you will, had left her body and gone elsewhere.

Cade had no doubt that he was looking at it now.

"Oh, you bastard," he said, surprised to find himself able to speak.

The Adversary just laughed.

"Will you do it? Will you open the door?"

Cade shook his head. "No."

The Adversary turned away from him and raised his hands. Power flashed, but Cade didn't know what it was for. A few moments passed and then from out of the ruins stumbled Riley. He was clearly not under his own power; his steps uncertain, his direction shaky. In one hand he held his sword. His struggle to free himself could easily be seen on his face, though when he, in turn, saw Cade that struggle changed to simple fear.

They were out of their league and Riley knew it.

As Cade watched, Riley's gaze shifted past the spot where Cade was secured to the remains of the wall and his expression changed to one of bewilderment. The sound of someone approaching reached Cade and then moved passed him.

Duncan stepped into view.

His eyes were empty, his face slack-jawed, and yet he moved forward with purpose and grace. In one hand he held a combat knife and there was no evidence of the injuries that had forced him to clamber along wearily behind Bishop.

Duncan marched forward, moving inexorably closer to Riley, brandishing his weapon.

"Cade?" Riley called, clearly uncertain what to do.

But when he tried to answer, the head of Echo Team discovered that while he might be able to move his head, his voice had been taken from him.

"Cade, help me!" Riley called, as Duncan moved closer.

The Adversary stepped in front of Cade, blocking his view.

"Open the door and I will free your friends."

Cade shook his head.

"Very well. Let it be on your hands."

The Adversary waved his hand in Riley's direction and then stepped aside to enjoy the show.

Unable to do anything, Cade was forced to watch as his two comrades attacked each other against their will.

Neither of the men was interested in defense and both took horrendous blows as they fought without consideration of their own safety. In seconds, they had each sustained grievous wounds and were bleeding in half a dozen places.

"Shall I stop?" asked the Adversary.

Cade struggled to speak, to tell the Adversary that he'd do it, that he'd open the damned doorway, but the other refused to release his arcane hold on Cade's vocal chords. The Adversary was enjoying this and had no intention of stopping, Cade realized.

Even as he fought against the bonds that held him, Cade saw Riley thrust his sword forward, impaling Duncan through the stomach, the point of his weapon emerging from the younger Templar's lower back. At the same time, Duncan's hand came swinging around and embedded his knife deep in Riley's unprotected neck.

Cade watched in horror as both men toppled to the ground, unmoving.

Silence fell.

To be broken a moment later by the Adversary's cackling laughter.

"Oh, what a show! What a show!" the fiend said, smiling all the while.

Cade vomited in helpless fear and emotional pain.

But the Adversary wasn't done. The fallen angel had one more offer to make.

"Obviously, the stick didn't seem to work. Maybe you are

more a carrot kind of guy." The Adversary moved closer and whispered in Cade's ear.

"How about I return your wife to you? Restore her to how see was on that day before I entered your lives? You could hold her again. Hear her voice. See her smile. Make love to her as if all this never happened. All you need to do is open that doorway and carry her back across the Veil. Reuniting her spirit with her body will return her to the way she was all those years before. It will be like all this had never happened."

And to his shame, Cade was tempted.

Why not? he thought. *Why not give Gabrielle another chance at life? After all, wasn't that what he'd wanted all along? Wasn't that why he'd joined the Order in the first place? Wasn't that why he'd spent so many years, so much time and determination learning everything he could about the Adversary and the world beyond the barrier, so much time searching for his wife once he'd realized that she wasn't at rest in the afterlife?*

The Adversary stared at him, the hint of a smile forming at the corners of his mouth, as if he could hear what Cade was thinking.

That did it. It was like a bucket of cold water being thrown in Cade's face. He knew there had to be something more to it. The Adversary would never give anyone a moment of happiness when he could create a moment of misery instead. Cade understood that instinctively. So what was it?

Cade looked toward Gabrielle, pretending to be considering the Adversary's offer while he racked his mind for an answer to the puzzle. Clearly the Adversary was capable of entering the real world on his own; Cade had seen him there on more than one occasion, including the day he'd murdered Gabrielle. So it wasn't that. It had to be something more.

Could it be something to do with the nature of the Beyond itself? Cade thought furiously. *Could that be it?*

He glanced upward at the churning tear in the sky above him.

Standing in front of him, the Adversary followed his gaze and sad, "Yes, yes that's right. You can do it. Take your wife back. Open the gateway." His voice dripped with eagerness and desire.

Cade ignored him, thinking furiously. What would happen if he opened a gate of that size? What would it do to the corresponding location on the other side? What would it be like to be standing there when the gate opened?

Probably be hell itself, he mused, and then he had it.

Hell itself. That was it!

Opening a gate of that size would create an imbalance between the two worlds, an imbalance Cade had no doubt that the Adversary would capitalize on, that he would use his own powers to warp and expand. If the Adversary tore a big enough hole in the barrier that separated the two states of reality, that barrier would more likely than not start to fail at a greater rate, becoming larger, until it ceased to exist at all.

The real world and the Beyond would cease to exist as separate locations, but mix together, becoming one.

Hell on earth was right.

That was the answer.

But would that be so bad? he wondered. *With Gabrielle at your side once more, would anything else matter?*

He never had the chance to answer that question.

Motion behind the Adversary caught his eye.

CHAPTER 35

"BENEATH A TEAR IN THE SKY"

A FIGURE WAS RISING UP behind the Adversary, its features shrouded in dust and shadow. Cade strained to see who or what it was, convinced that he was about to meet another of the Adversary's seemingly endless list of inhuman allies, and was shocked to realize that it was Duncan.

He was still alive!

Duncan's lips were set in a grim line and it was obvious to Cade that he was at the end of his rope. Summoning the strength just to stand looked as if it had been almost too much for him and yet there he was, doggedly moving toward the Adversary. His lips were moving, more than likely in prayer, and as Cade watched the younger knight extended his hands out before him, palms upright and facing in the Adversary's direction. Cade engaged his Sight and through it he could see the blue witchfire that sprang up between Duncan's fingertips, flowing down to gather in a pool at the center of each palm. Cade knew he was seeing the physical manifestation of Duncan's healing power, but he didn't understand just what his teammate hoped to accomplish with it. Duncan couldn't use it on himself or he certainly would have done so before now and Cade was too far away for Duncan to reach.

Which left only the Adversary.

Seeing his teammate's determination was enough to reinvigorate Cade's own resistance and he struggled anew against the invisible bonds that held him as securely as the iron shackles that Duncan still wore on his wrists. Cade threw everything he had into the attempt, straining his body, flexing his muscles, willing himself to move, but it was no use.

He was trapped.

Duncan had closed the distance to the Adversary while Cade had been struggling and with a shout of defiance, he slammed his hands against the enemy's back.

Power flashed, filling the night air like a thousand incandescent flares set off at the same time, enveloping the three of them in a shimmering ball of arcane energy that hissed and spit and crackled with a voice all its own.

Over the Adversary's shoulder, Cade could see Duncan. His head was bowed and his eyes were closed as he poured every ounce of energy he had into the link that he'd established with the fallen angel in front of him.

With a flash of insight, Cade understood.

The Adversary was corrupt right down to the very core of his being, but he hadn't been created that way. Once, long ago, he had been the angel Asharael, fashioned as an agent of goodness by the hand of God himself, a living collection of purity and grace and divine power, all bound up inside a frame designed specifically to accomplish the Lord's will. Somewhere along the way Asharael had lost his way. His soul had grown sick, infected with the rot and pain and shame of this fallen world. Duncan apparently believed that what had been created for good could be healed of the evil that had taken it over, could be returned to its original nature and form.

Power poured forth from Duncan's hands in a wave, washing up and over the Adversary's form one slow inch at a time. Wherever it touched the other's flesh bulged and shook and shivered, the divine presence summoned by Duncan's healing talent meeting the corruption that filled the enemy's body, mind, and soul. The Adversary's eyes bulged, his hands danced, and his feet beat a rhythmic tattoo against the ground beneath them as if in response to a beat that only they could hear.

In that split second, the Adversary's hold on Cade was broken.

The invisible bonds that had been holding him in place abruptly disappeared as the Adversary was forced to use all of his concentration and energy to defend against Duncan's attack.

Cade crashed to the ground.

Time slowed to a crawl.

It was as if Cade was suddenly standing in the spaces between each moment, able to see and hear and feel a thousand times faster than those around him, like time had been lain at his feet to do with as he would.

He looked past the confrontation to where his wife's body lay on the stone bier. He wanted so badly to see her sit up and rise off that stone platform, longed to hold her in his arms and to hear her sweet voice again. The Adversary's offer to return her to him was more tempting than he wanted to admit, even to himself, but the cost…the cost was just too high. How could he look her in the eyes and tell her that he'd selfishly given up the entire world and everyone in it just to spend another day with her? How could he trade all of humanity, its past, present and future, for his own happiness?

He couldn't.

Everything in his heart and soul cried out against it. He'd seen the evil that a lesser angel like Baraquel could inflict on those around him while constrained by the boundaries of the Veil. To tear down that barrier, to let the Adversary loose in the world with all of his infernal powers intact and at his disposal, powers that made the things Baraquel could do look like the antics of a circus clown, was unthinkable.

He cast a last glance in her direction. A whispered, "I'm sorry, Gabrielle," fell from his lips and then he scrambled to his feet. His sword still lay on the ground nearby and he dove for it now, knowing it was his only chance of surviving what was to come.

His hand closed about the hilt just the Adversary let out a roar that literally shook the ground beneath their feet.

Cade spun around.

The Adversary was now face-to-face with Duncan and Cade was just in time to see the creature shove his hands wrist-deep in the center of Duncan's unprotected chest.

The young Templar's eyes gaped open in shock and a thick stream of blood erupted from his open mouth.

The Adversary's triumphant laughter filled the night air.

The sound galvanized Cade into action.

He charged forward and rammed his sword deep into the Adversary's back, right between the tattered remnants of his wings.

CHAPTER 36

"AT WORLD'S END"

C ADE'S SWORD SANK TO THE hilt in the Adversary's back, emerging from the other side and almost impaling Duncan. The Adversary shrieked in rage and pain, throwing Duncan to the side as he reached behind him, trying to reach the hilt and draw the weapon free. Black blood poured from his mouth and nose in a seeming torrent.

Aware that he had only seconds in which to act, Cade spun on his heel and rushed over to where Riley's body lay. His teammate's hand still held his sword and that was what Cade was after.

But when he tried to free it from his friend's grasp, Riley's fingers clenched around it.

Cade's gaze went from the sword to Riley's face.

His eyes were open and moving slightly. Duncan's knife was still embedded deep in his throat, and blood was everywhere, but amazingly the Templar warrior was still clinging to life, refusing to die.

Riley was alive!

The realization rocked Cade to his core and created even more urgency, if that was at all possible. If he could deal with the Adversary and return them to the other side close enough to get Riley help, he might just survive.

He grabbed Riley's arm.

"Listen to me, Matt. I'm going to get us out of here, but I need your sword to do it. Let go!"

The other man did so.

"Hold on. I'll be right back for you."

Standing, he turned his back on his friend to face his enemy.

The Adversary had both his hands on the sword where it emerged from his stomach and was slowly pushing back inside his body, forcing it out in the direction it had come.

Cade was all but out of time.

Still, he had to try.

He rushed forward, his feet pounding against the scorched earth beneath them, his breath echoing in his ears, his heart hammering in his chest.

The Adversary gave a final shove and Cade's sword popped free and fell to the ground at his feet.

He turned, his bloodied hands rising, preparing to unleash another wave of arcane power in Cade's direction.

"Not this time, asshole," Cade said and brought Riley's sword down.

The Adversary's severed head flipped through the air, hit the ground, and rolled several times before coming to stop, looking back in Cade's direction.

For a moment his lips seemed to move, as if he were still speaking, and then the fallen angel's body burst into brilliant flames, burning so brightly that Cade was forced to shield his eyes and turn away from its brilliance to keep from being wounded himself.

When he looked back again, the Adversary was gone.

So was Gabrielle.

The bier on which her spirit had rested was empty.

Goodbye, my love, he thought, but then was forced to turn his back on the past in order to deal with the present. There would be time enough for grieving later. One look at Duncan told Cade that all he needed to know about the younger man's condition and so he rushed instead to Riley's side, determined to do what he could to save at least one of his friends.

EPILOGUE

A LMOST THREE DAYS LATER CADE climbed from the back of a taxi in the driveway of his home, exhausted and weary from all he'd been through. Cade paid the driver and then waited for him to turn around and leave the property before making his way inside the house.

Two months had passed since they had entered the Beyond. The Order had proclaimed them dead and had held burial ceremonies on their behalf, three empty coffins buried with full honors, despite Cade's prior conduct. He wondered how Riley would feel when he returned to the Newport Commandery and saw the headstone with his "death" date on it.

It had been close, there was no doubt about that. In the wake of the Adversary's destruction, Cade had found a smaller, more manageable portal and used that to transport an injured Riley back to the real world. By some miracle, and Cade had no doubt that it was divine intervention, there was no other explanation, they had appeared inside the barracks of the commandery in Arlington, Virginia. The locals had sprung into action, rushing Riley into surgery, and several hours later the doctor had emerged, telling Cade that Riley would pull through.

Cade had left a note for his brother in arms, telling him he'd be in touch, and then had gotten the hell out of there.

He dropped what little gear he had just inside the foyer and wandered through the kitchen to the back door. He stared across the yard at the workshop for a long moment, afraid to confront what he knew was waiting for him there.

Cade had been unable to reach Clearwater since his return, but he had no doubt the hedge witch had moved on to other issues. After all, he'd only hired her for a few days, not two months. He couldn't expect her to stick around. His only question was what she had done before leaving.

Had Clearwater left the wards up or had she disabled them? Would he find Gabrielle's body still intact, forever trapped in that nether world by the Adversary's sorcery, or would she have finally moved on to a better place, her body at long last beginning the decaying process that would return it to the earth from which it had been created, earth to earth, and dust to dust?

He didn't know.

But he couldn't put it off any longer; he had to find out.

He walked out of the house, crossed the yard, and stepped up to the workshop door.

Summoning his courage, he took a deep breath and went inside.

Made in the USA
Lexington, KY
16 November 2016